D0057133

You know you want to read
ALL the Pizza and Taco books!

WHO'S THE BEST?

BEST PARTY EVER!

SUPER-AWESOME COMIC!
(Coming in fall 2021)

BEST PARTY EVER!

STEPHEN SHASKAN

A STEPPING STONE BOOK™

Random House New York

To the most awesome Lilli B.

 Published in the United States by Random House Children's Books, a division of Penguin Random House LLC, New York.
Random House and the colophon are registered trademarks of Penguin Random House LLC.
Visit us on the Web! rhcbooks.com
Educators and librarians, for a variety of teaching tools, visit us at RHTeachersLibrarians.com

Library of Congress Cataloging-in-Publication Data is available upon request.
ISBN 978-0-593-12334-8 (trade) — ISBN 978-0-593-12335-5 (lib. bdg.) —
ISBN 978-0-593-12336-2 (ebook)

MANUFACTURED IN CHINA
10 9 8 7 6 5 4 3 2 1
First Edition

Contents

Chapter 1
What Do You Want to Do?

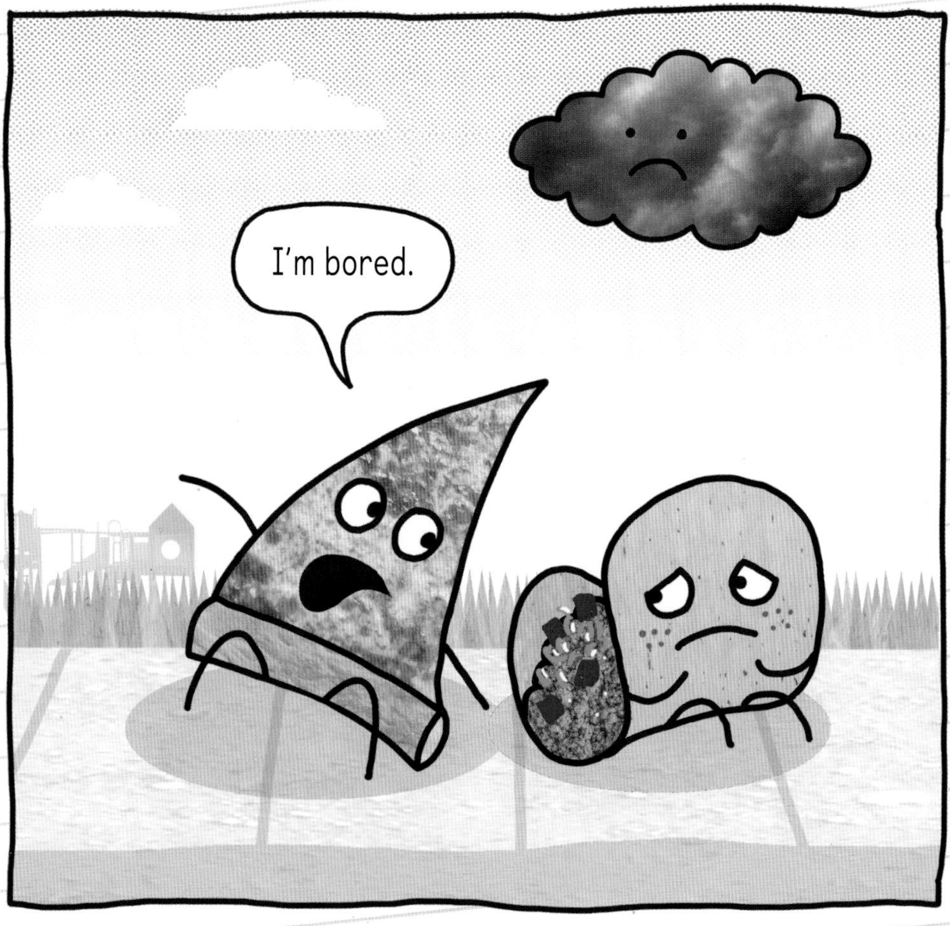
I'm bored.

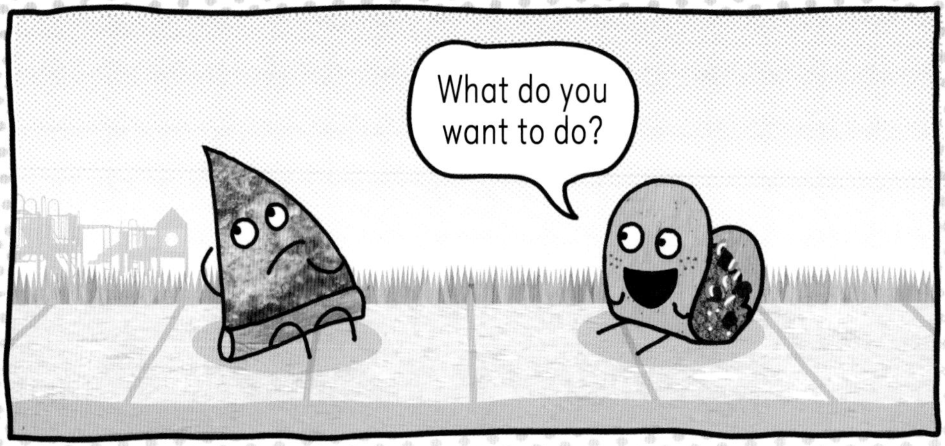
What do you want to do?

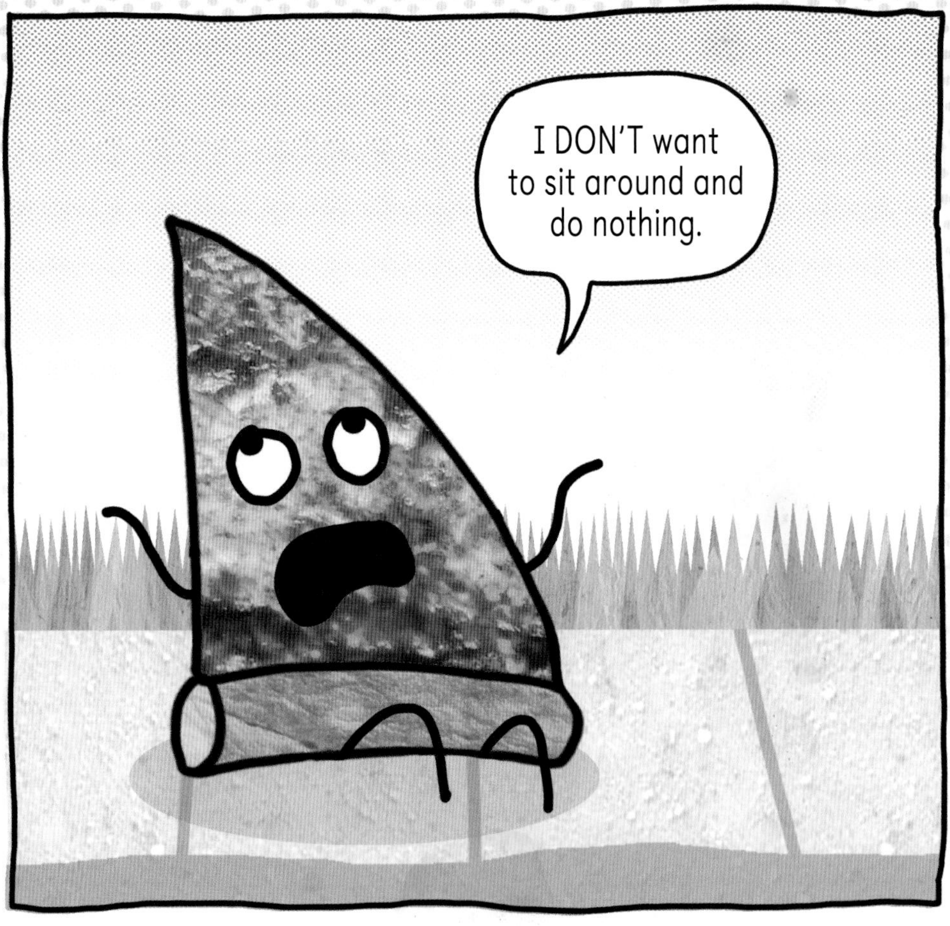
I DON'T want to sit around and do nothing.

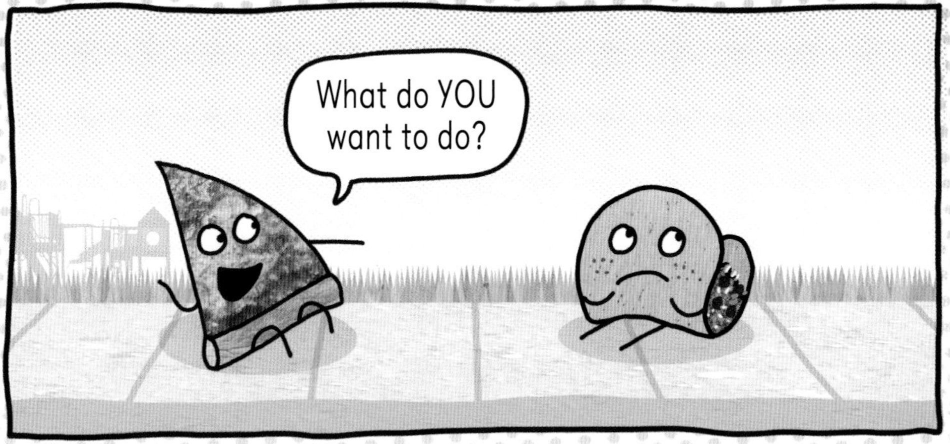
What do YOU want to do?

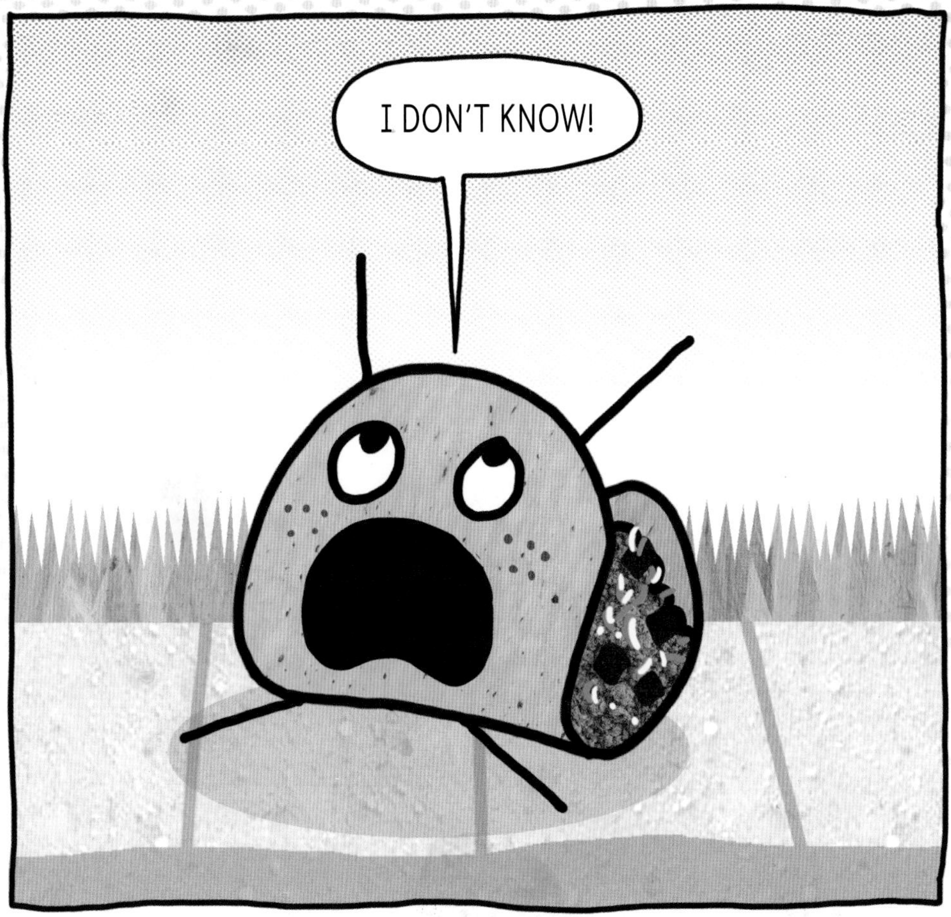
I DON'T KNOW!

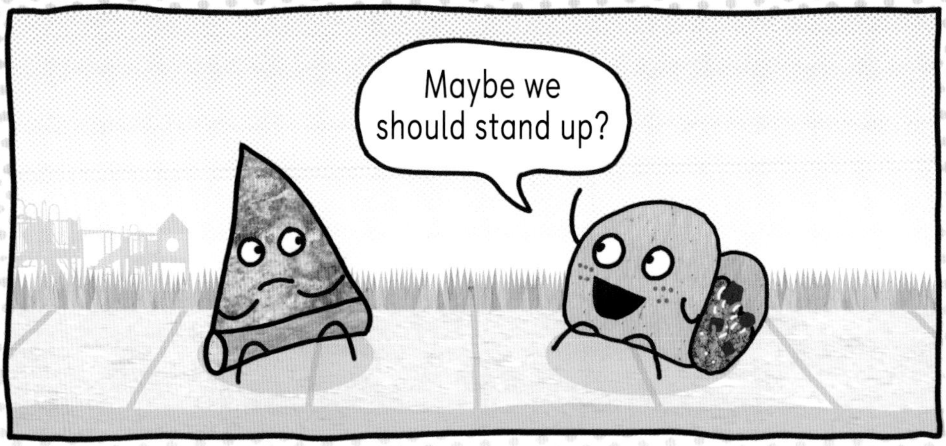
Maybe we should stand up?

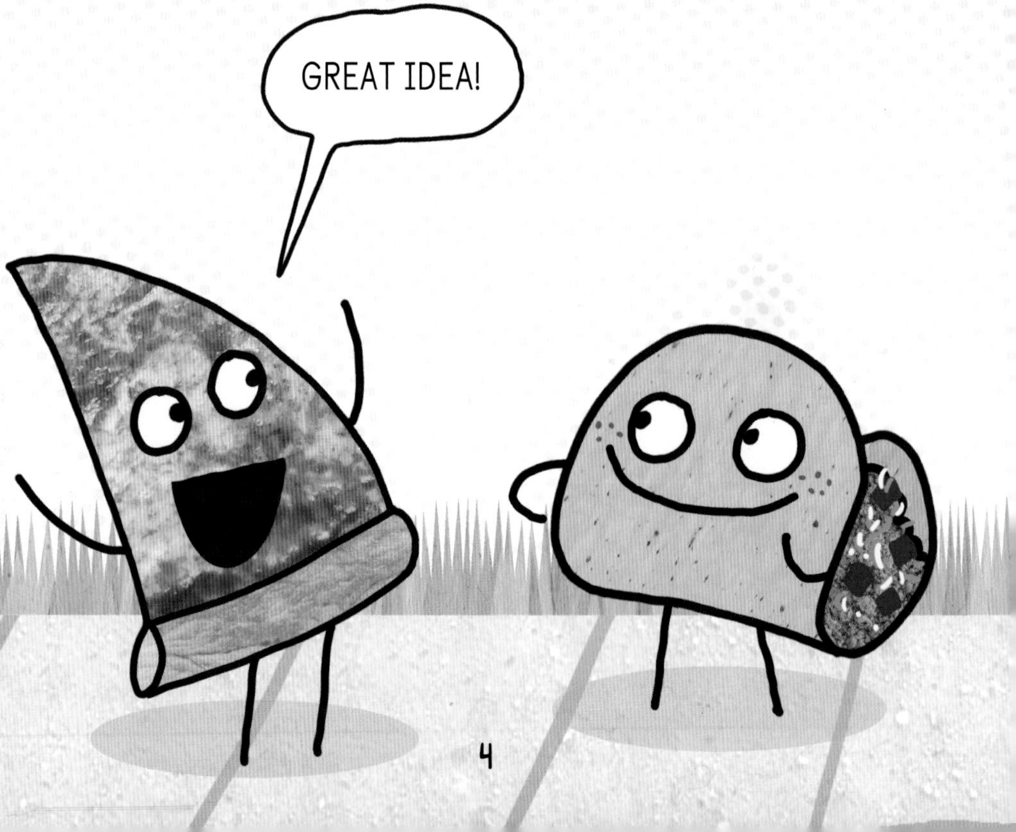
GREAT IDEA!

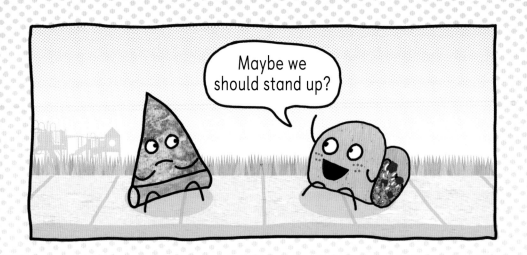

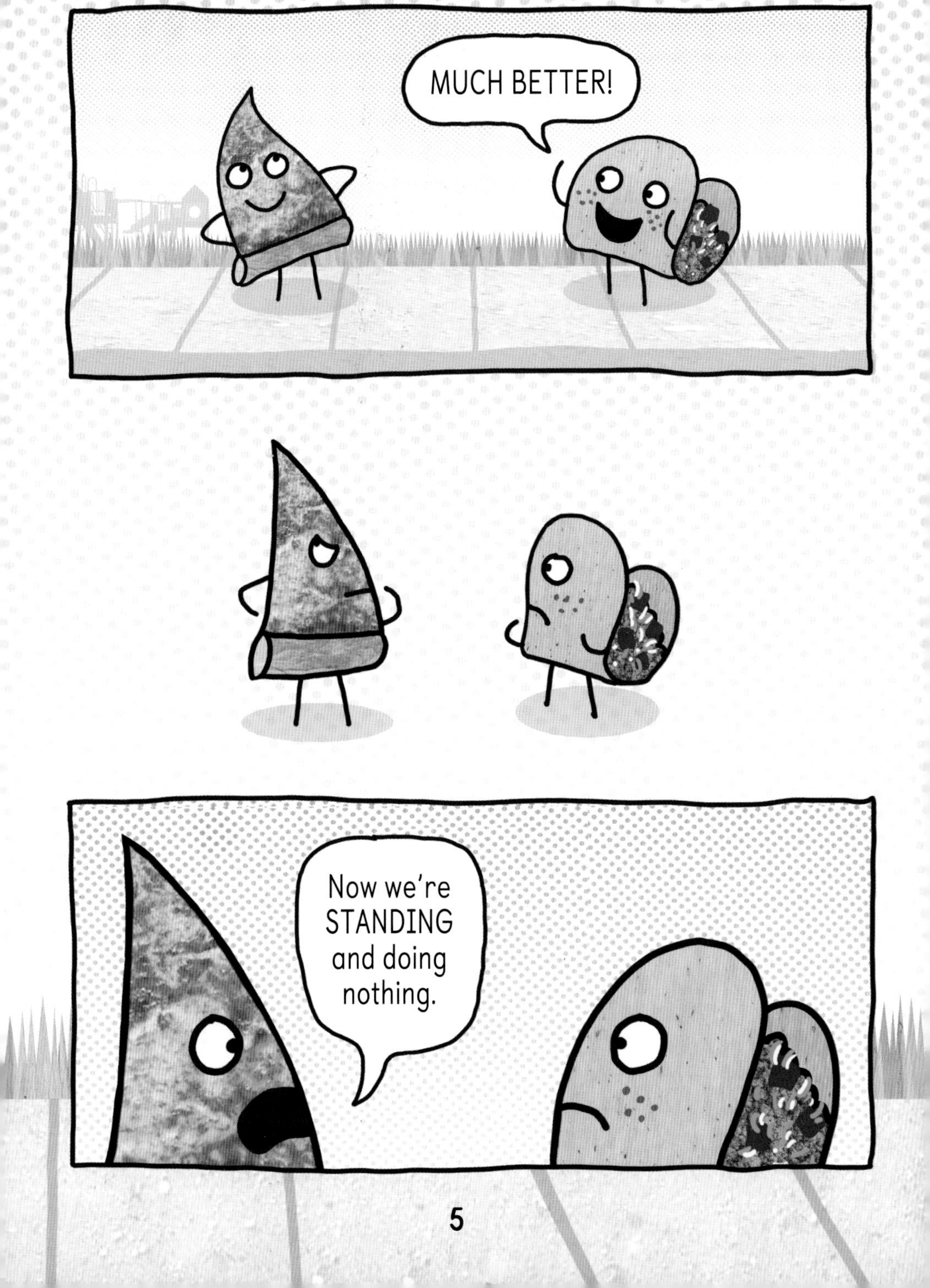
MUCH BETTER!
Now we're STANDING and doing nothing.

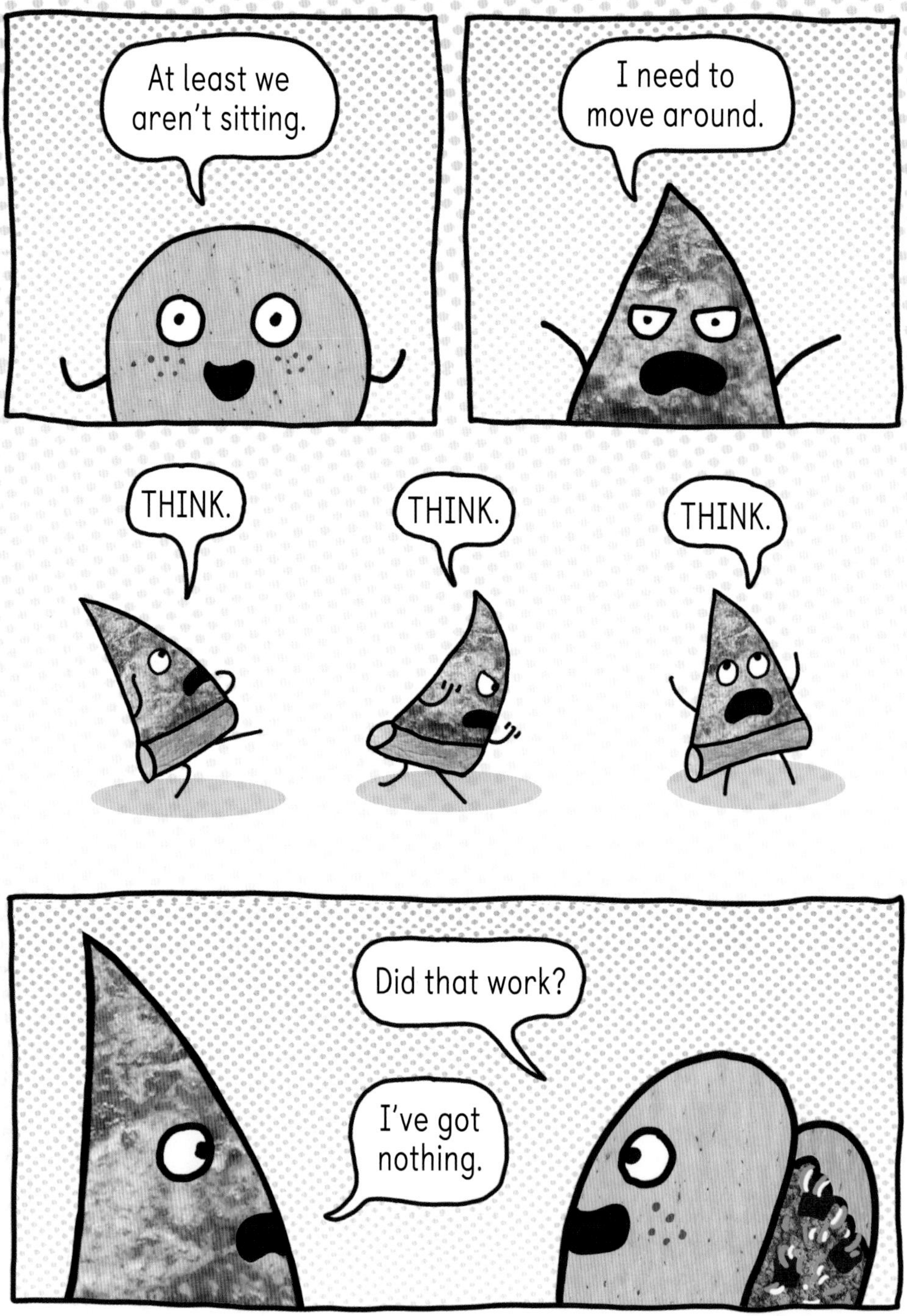
At least we aren't sitting.
I need to move around.
THINK.
THINK.
THINK.
Did that work?
I've got nothing.

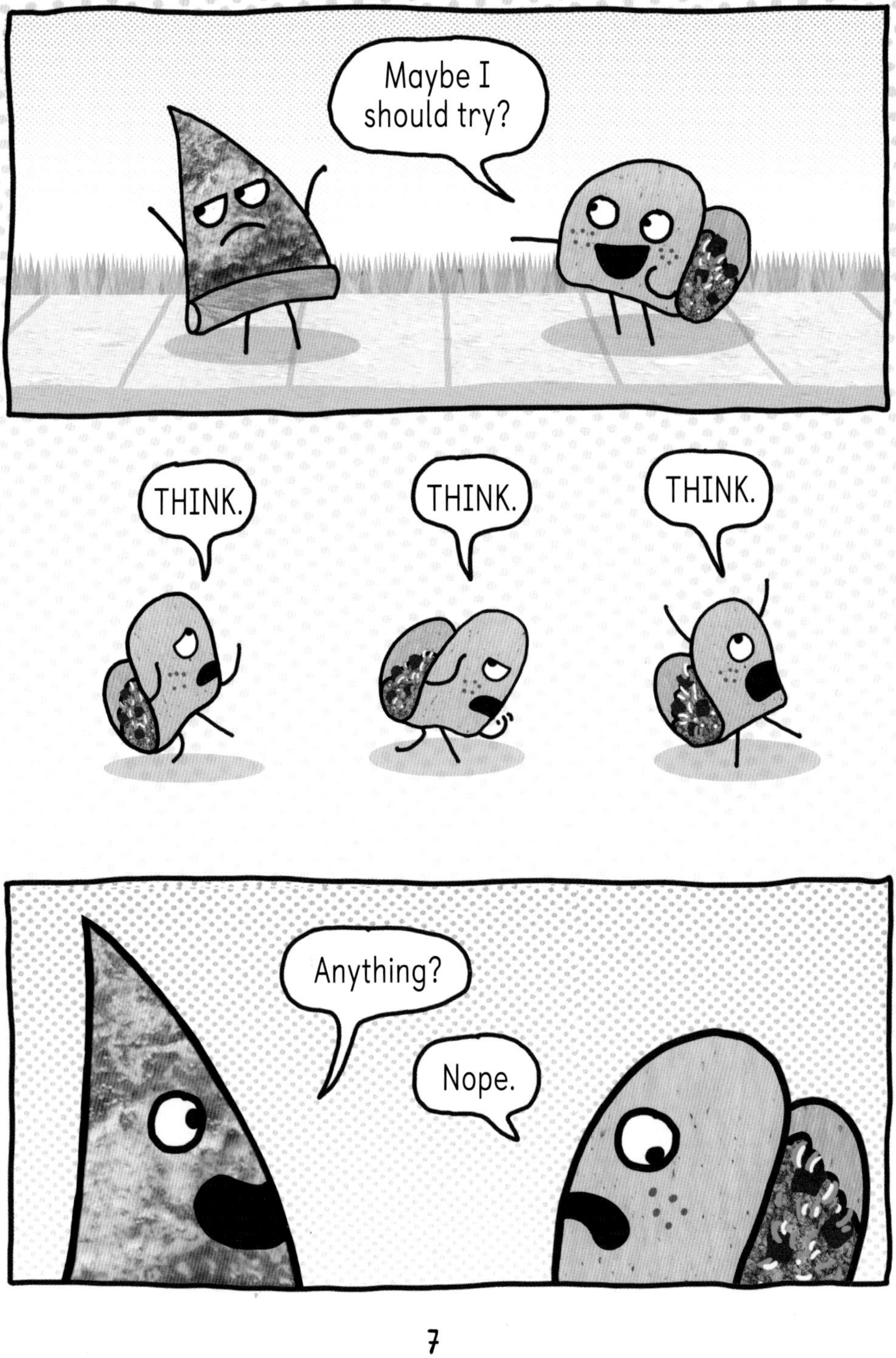
Maybe I should try?
THINK.
THINK.
THINK.
Anything?
Nope.

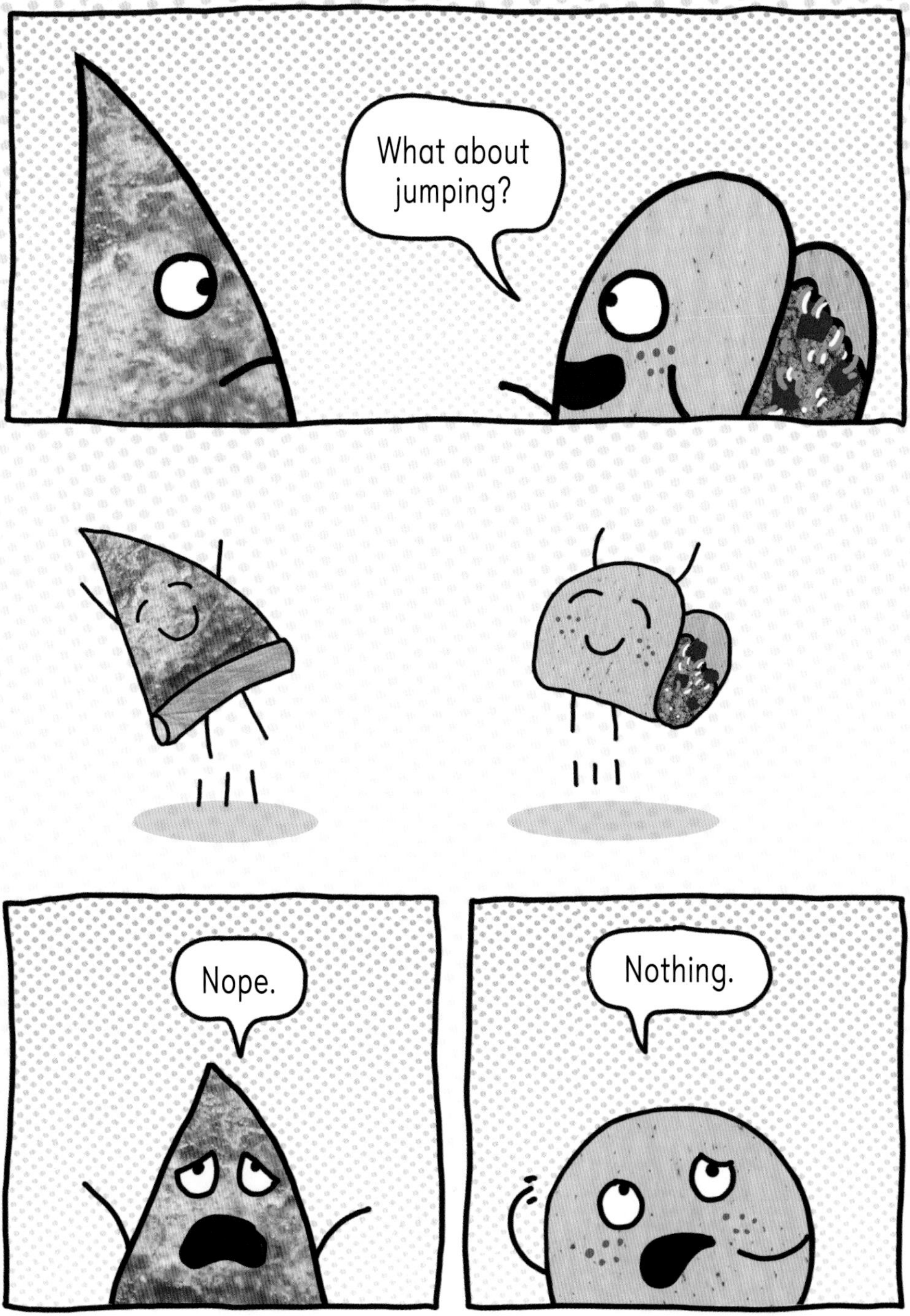
What about jumping?
Nope.
Nothing.

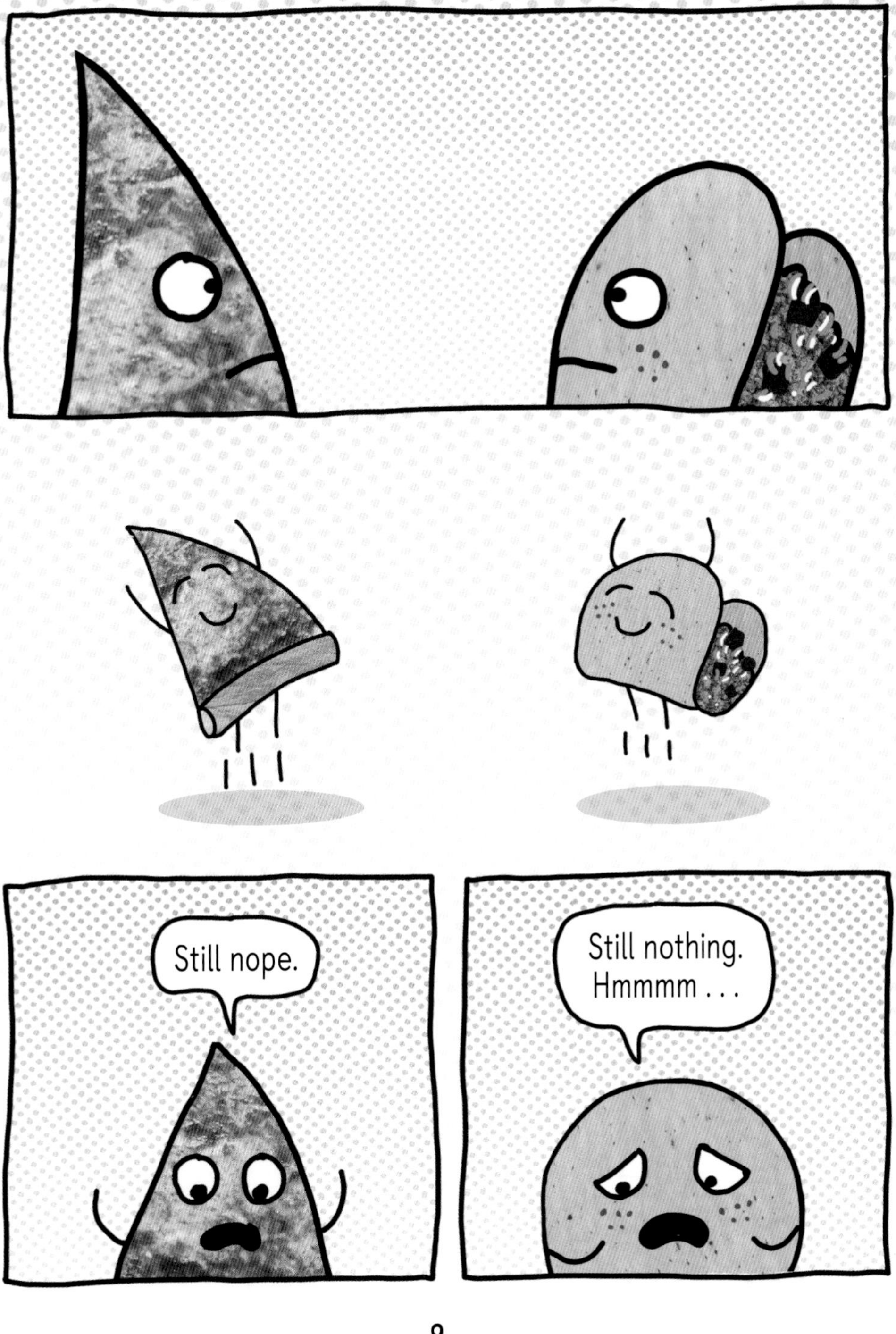
Still nope.
Still nothing. Hmmmm . . .

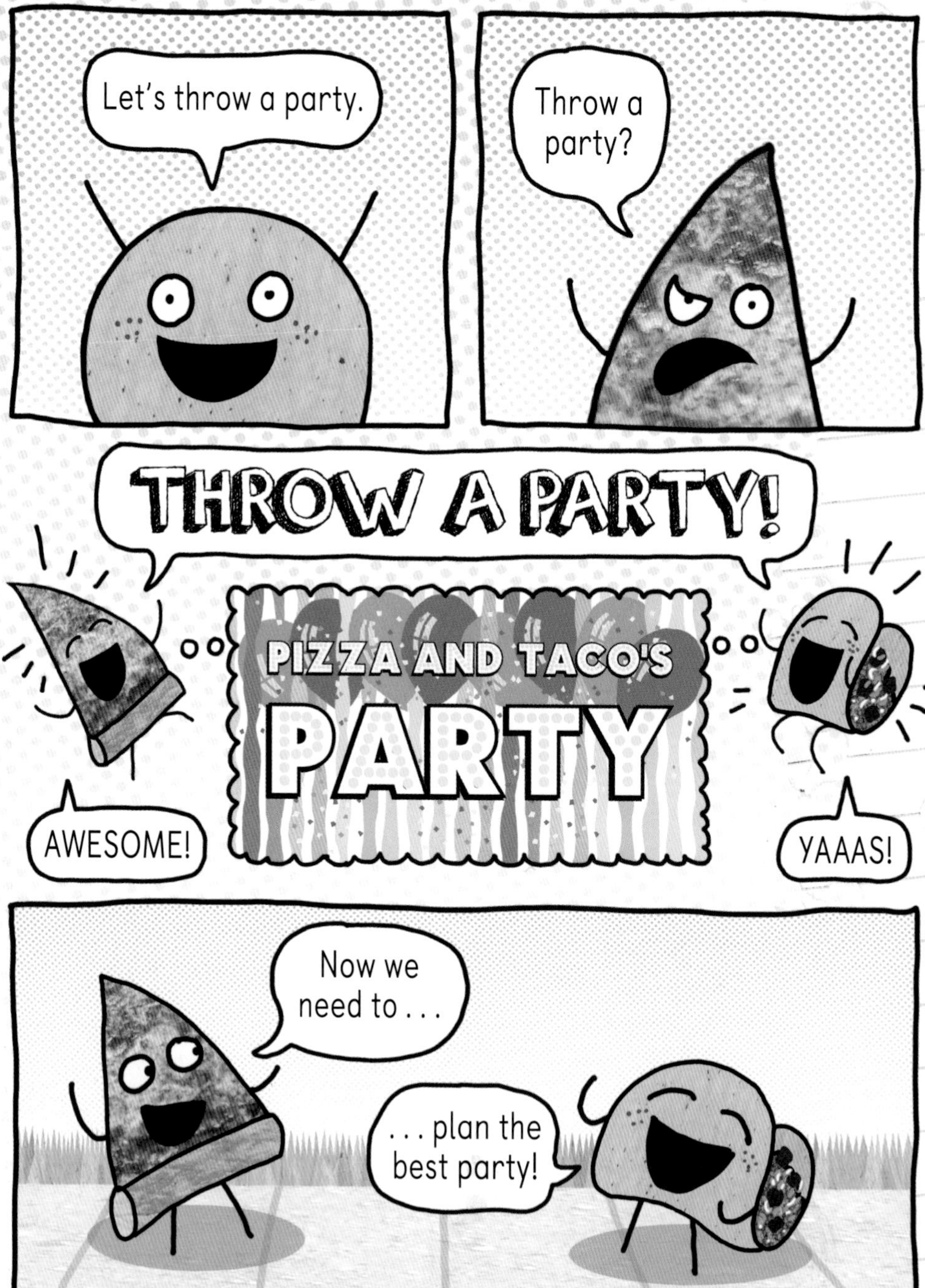
Let's throw a party.
Throw a party?
THROW A PARTY!
PIZZA AND TACO'S
PARTY
AWESOME!
YAAAS!
Now we need to . . .
. . . plan the best party!

Chapter 2
Pizza and Taco Plan the Best Party!

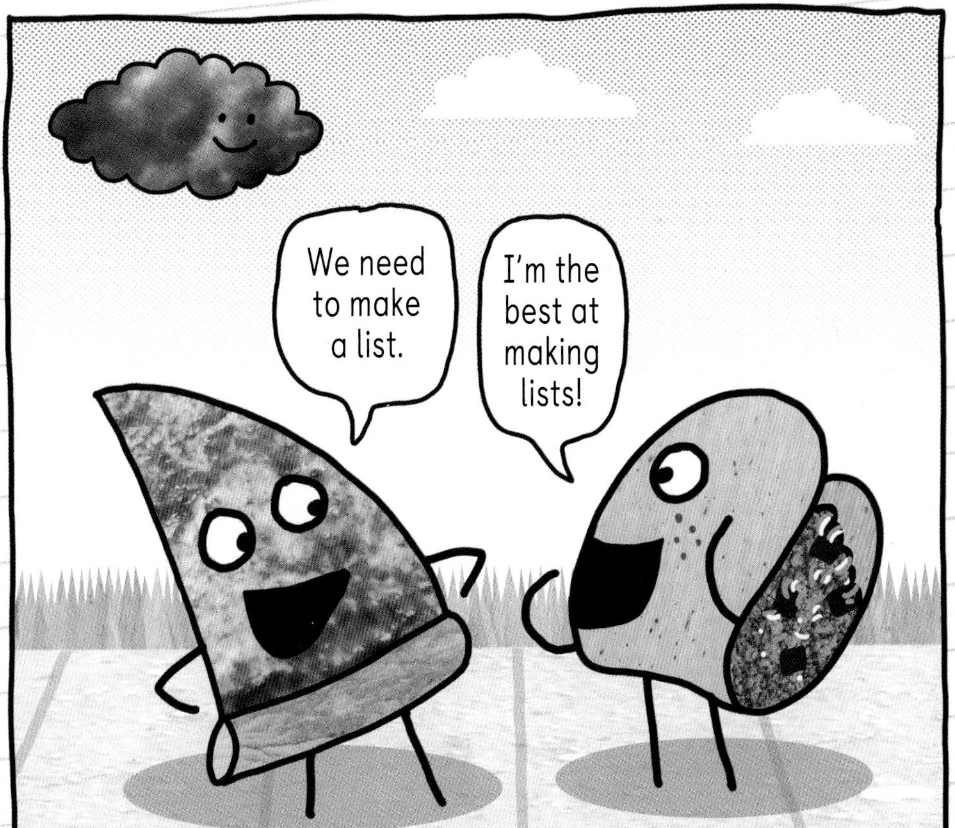
We need to make a list.
I'm the best at making lists!

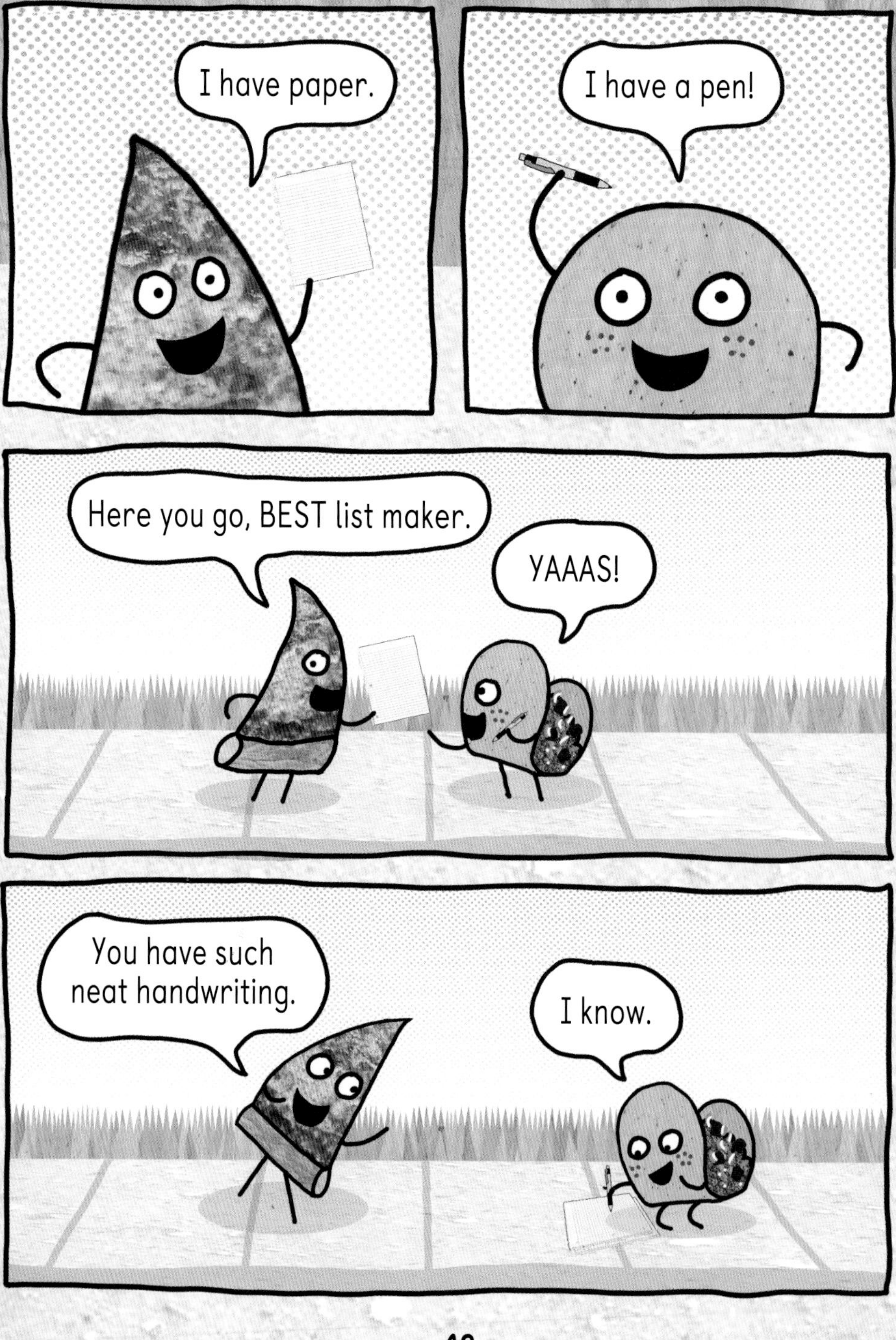
I have paper.
I have a pen!
Here you go, BEST list maker.
YAAAS!
You have such neat handwriting.
I know.

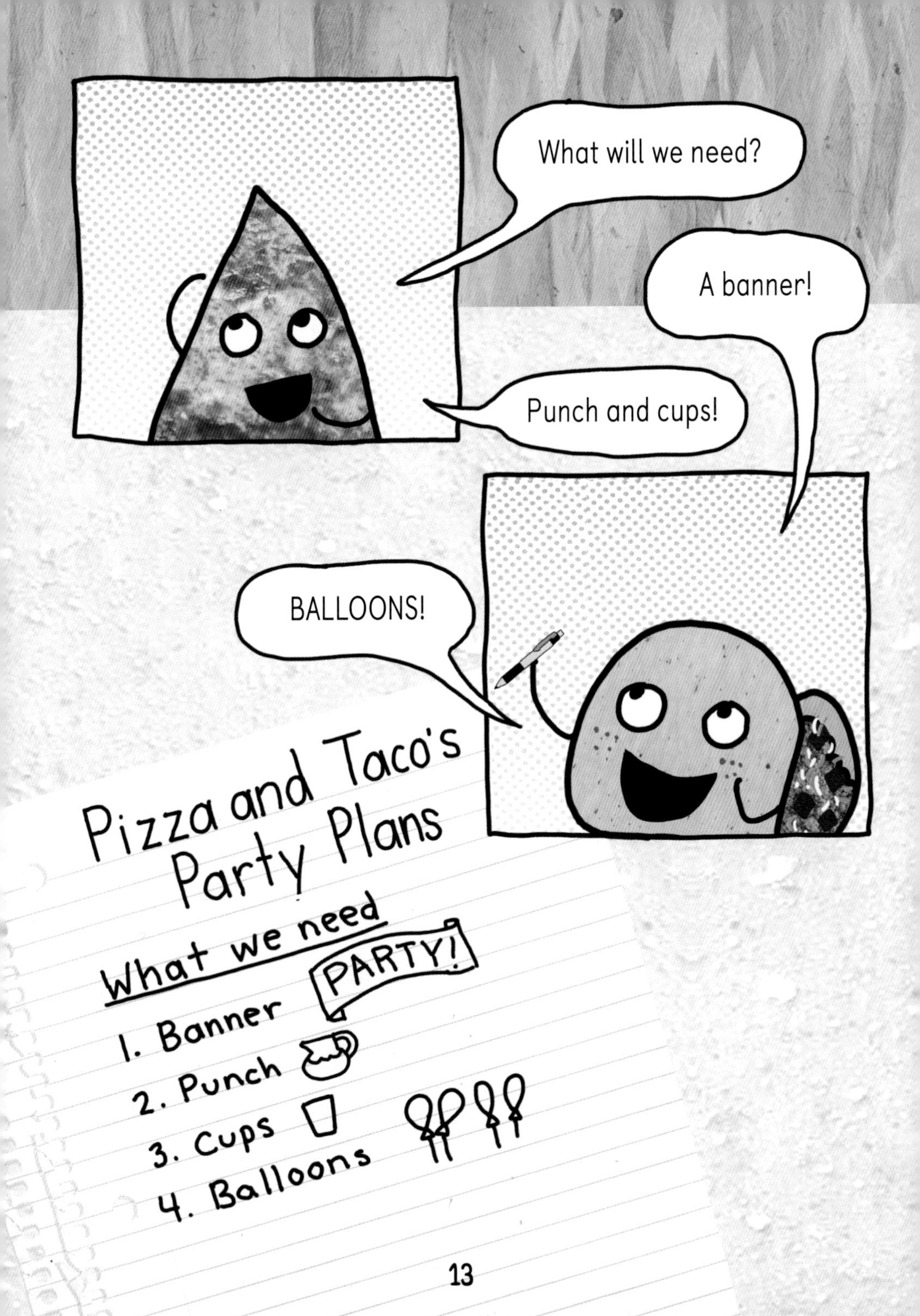
What will we need?
A banner!
Punch and cups!
BALLOONS!
Pizza and Taco's Party Plans
What we need
PARTY!
1. Banner
2. Punch
3. Cups
4. Balloons

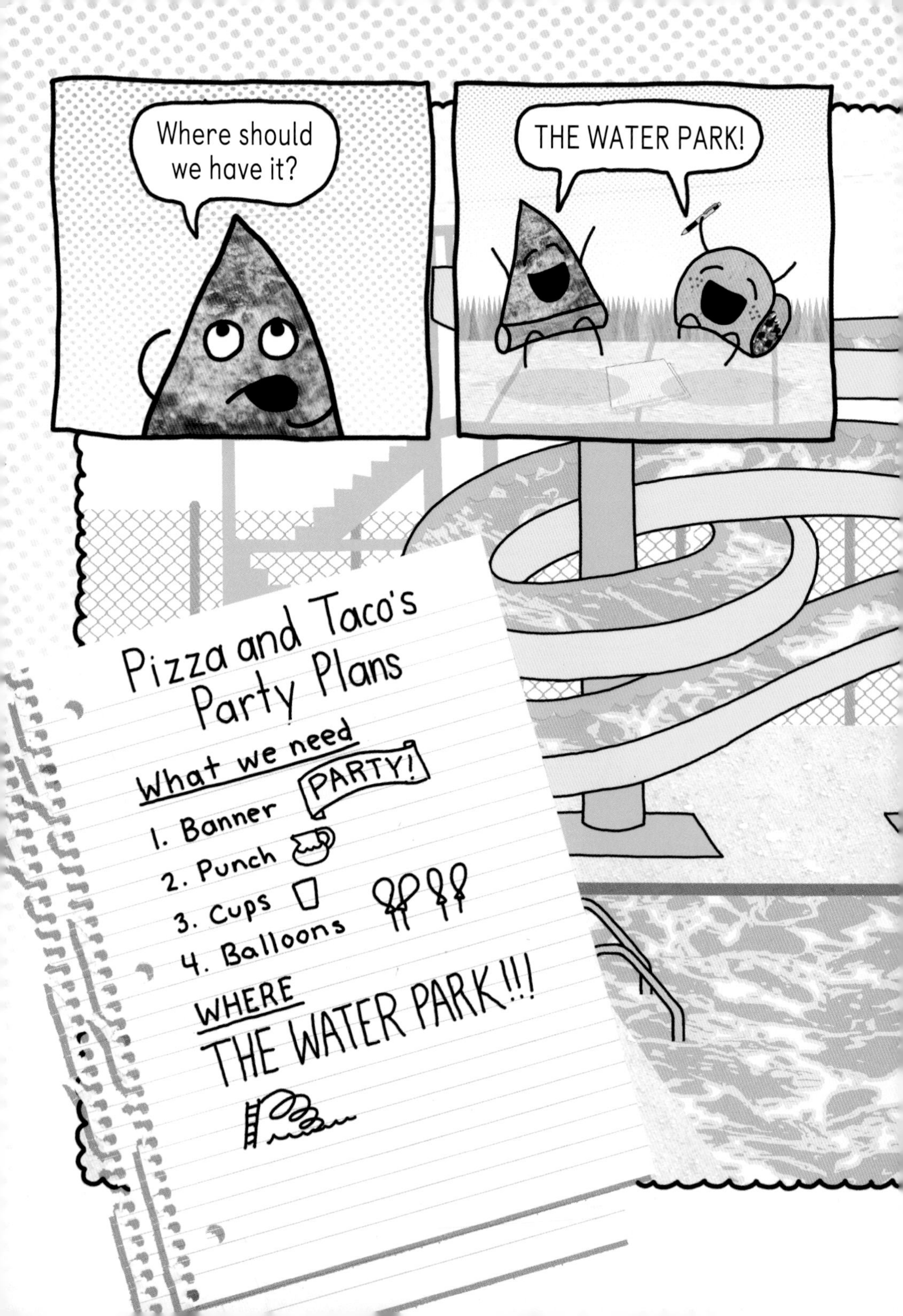

Where should we have it?
THE WATER PARK!
Pizza and Taco's Party Plans
What we need
1. Banner
PARTY!
2. Punch
3. Cups
4. Balloons
WHERE
THE WATER PARK!!!

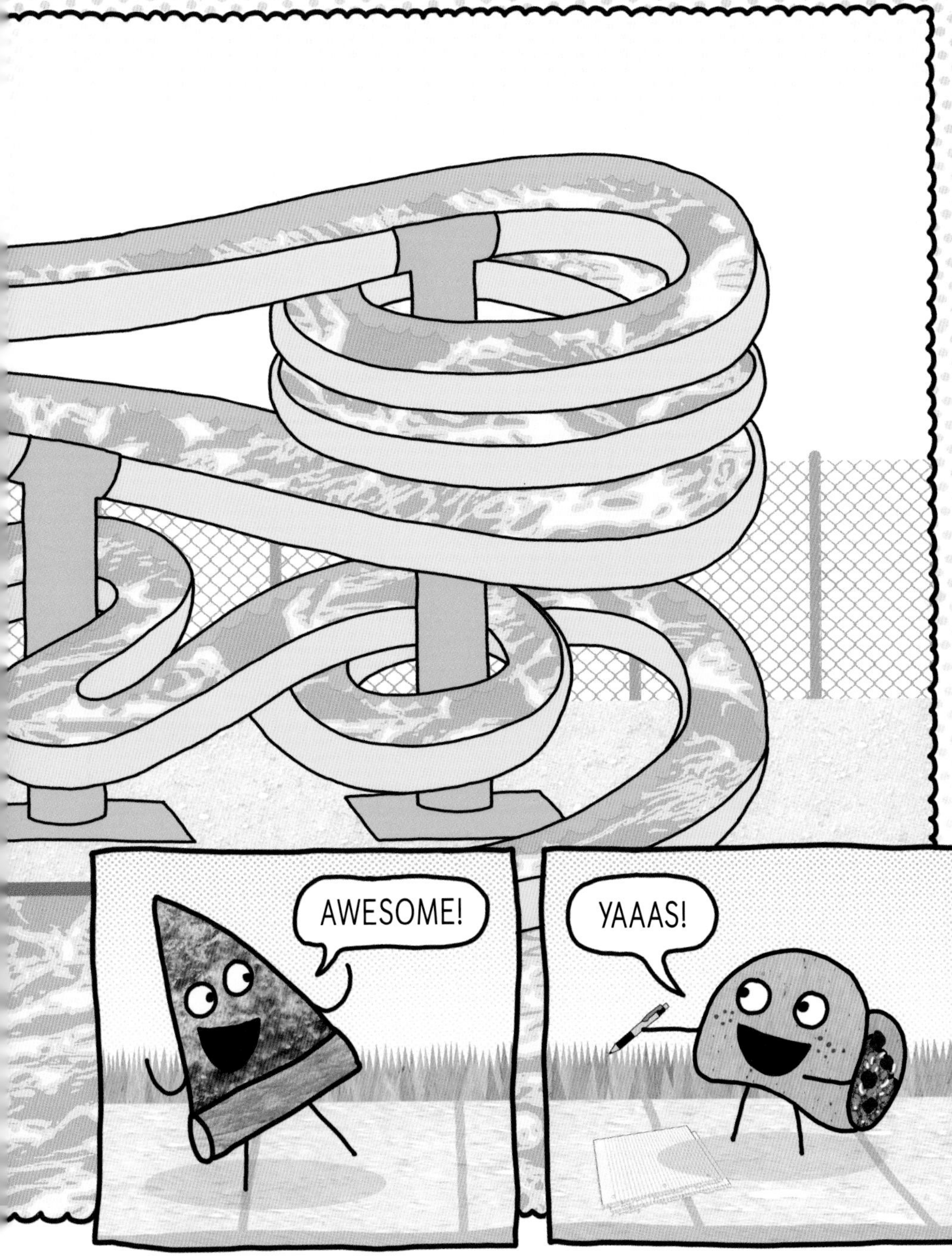
AWESOME!
YAAAS!

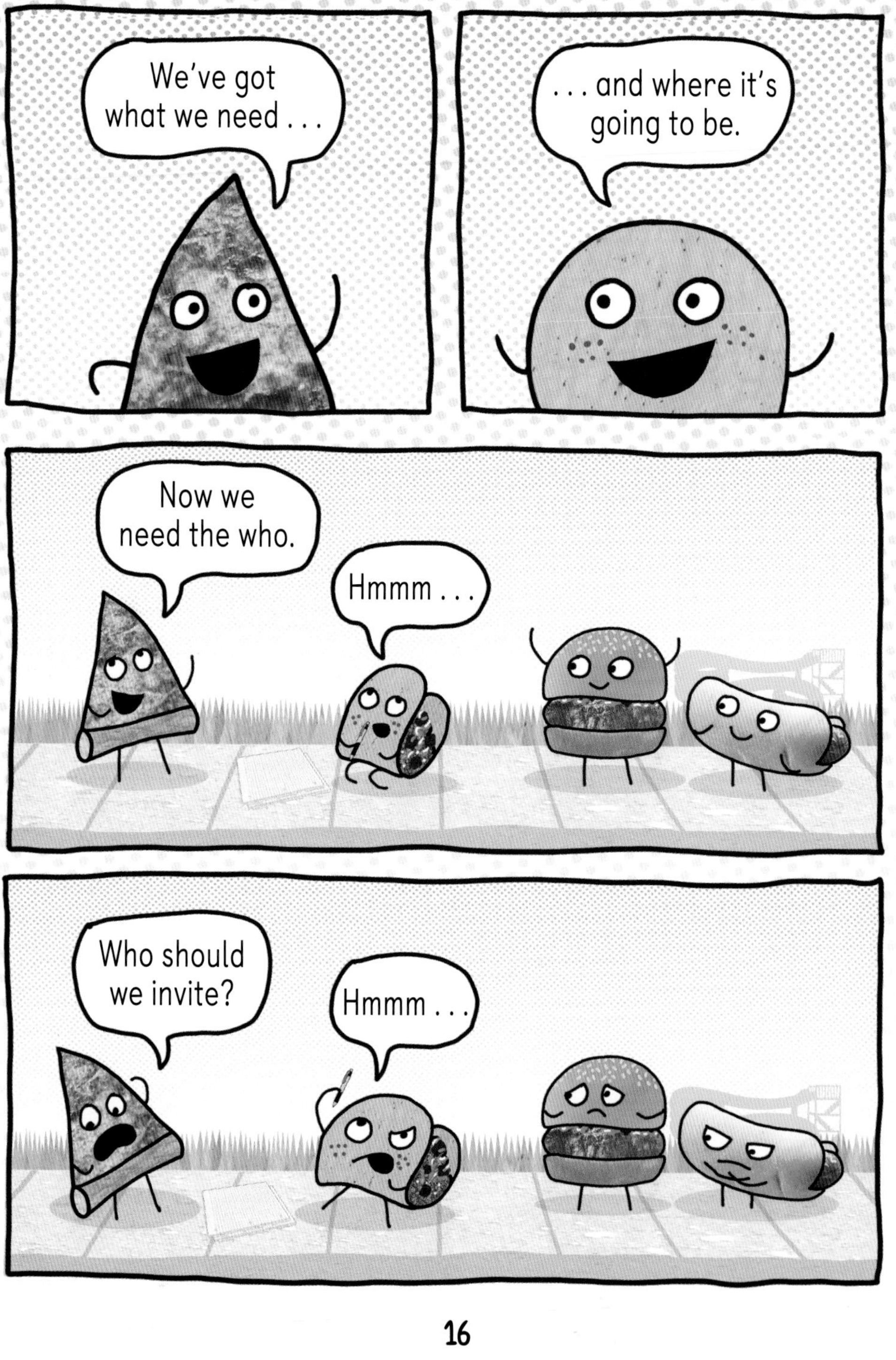
We've got what we need . . .
. . . and where it's going to be.
Now we need the who.
Hmmm . . .
Who should we invite?
Hmmm . . .

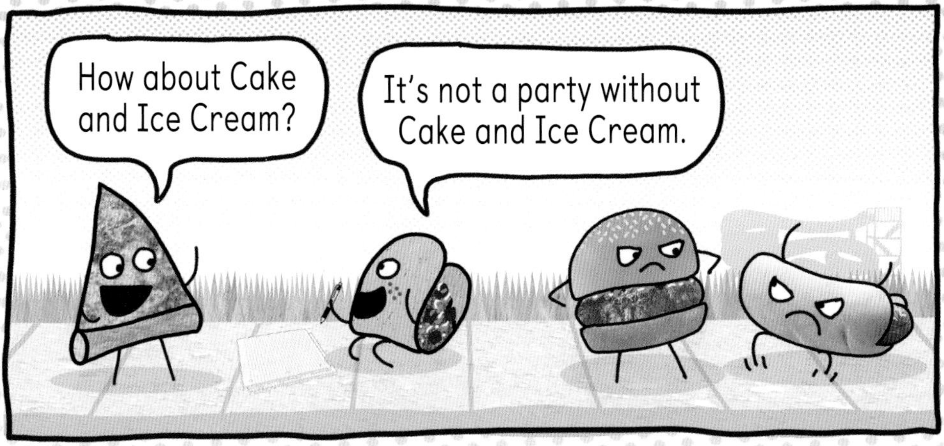
How about Cake and Ice Cream?
It's not a party without Cake and Ice Cream.

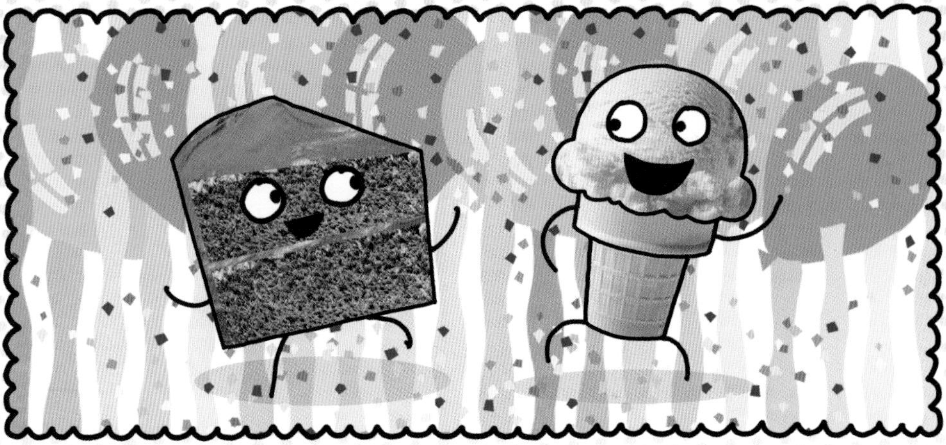

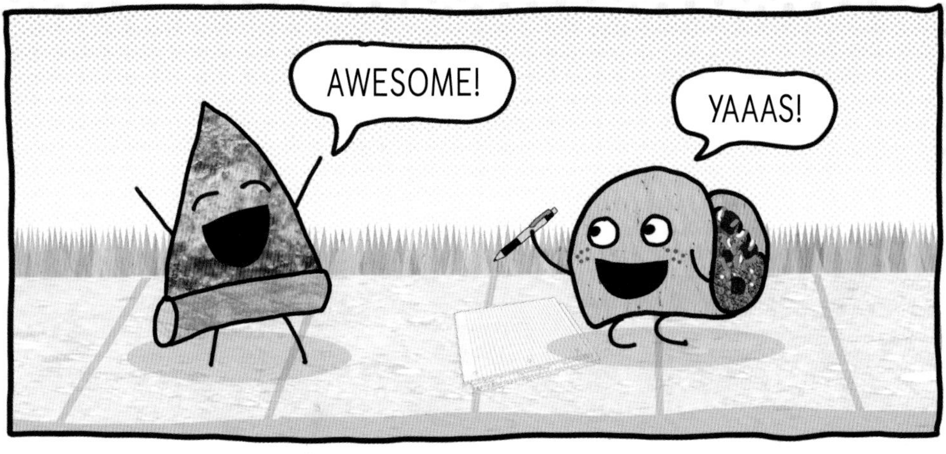
AWESOME!
YAAAS!

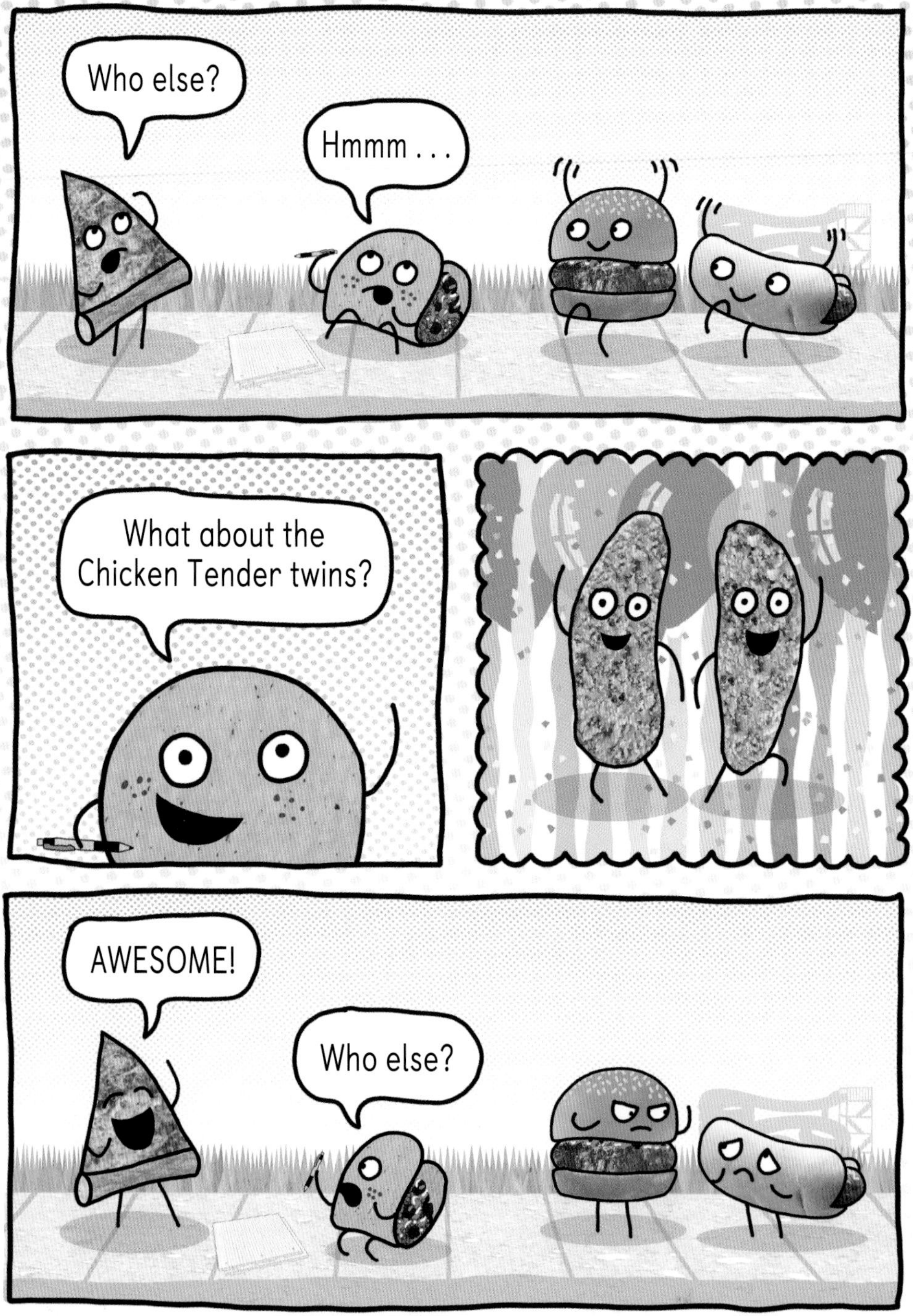
Who else?
Hmmm . . .
What about the Chicken Tender twins?
AWESOME!
Who else?

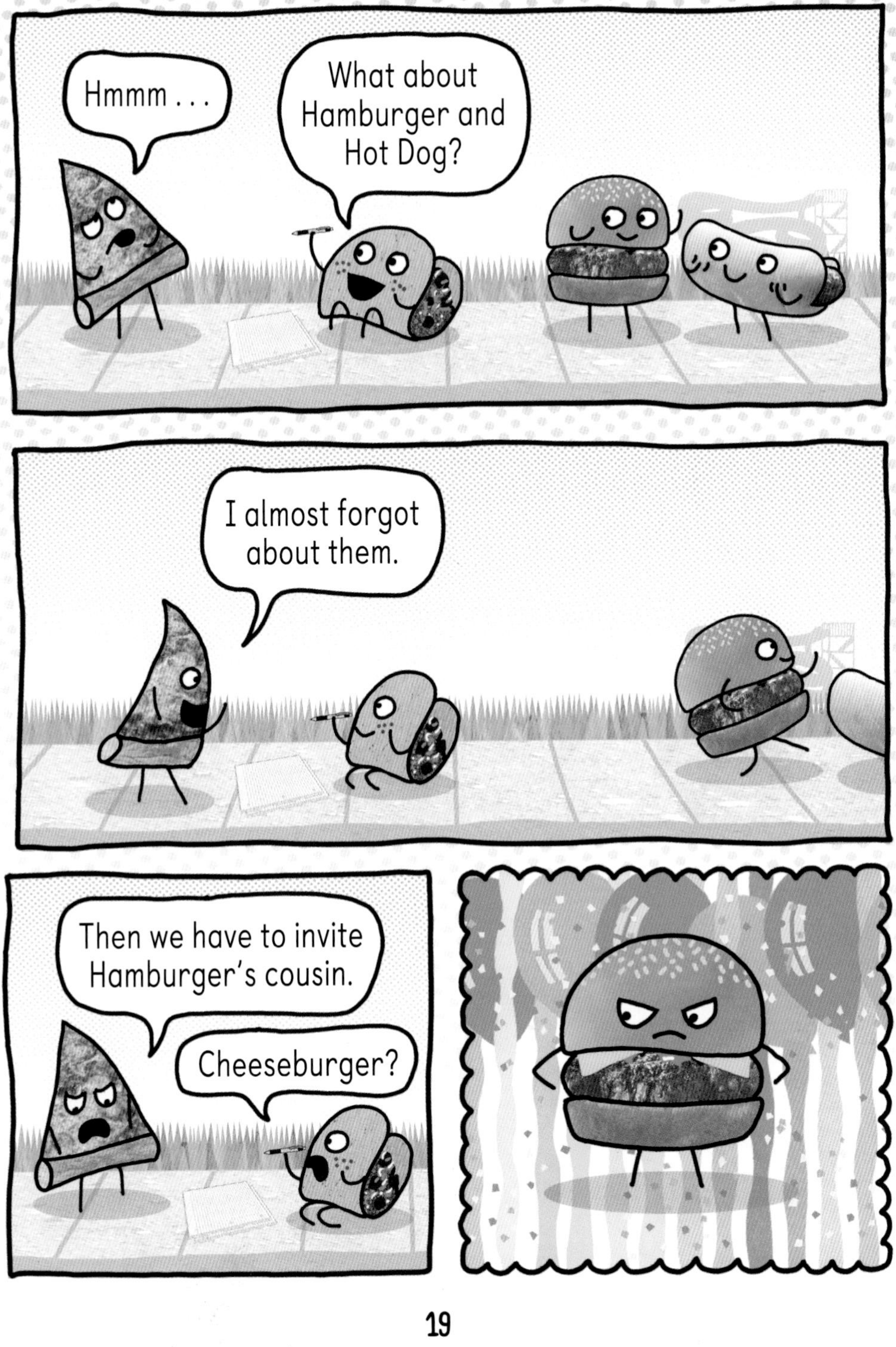
Hmmm . . .
What about Hamburger and Hot Dog?
I almost forgot about them.
Then we have to invite Hamburger's cousin.
Cheeseburger?

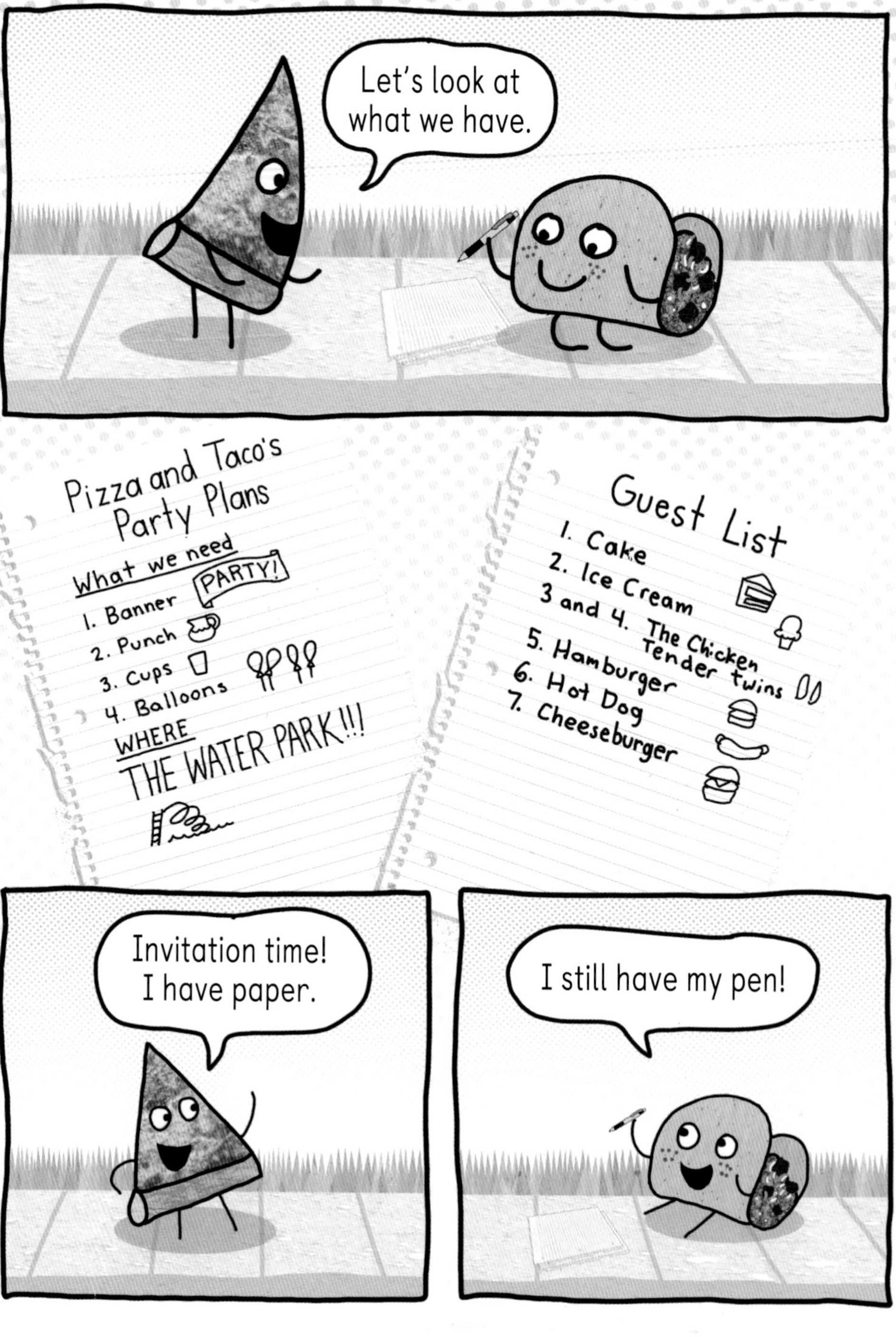
Let's look at what we have.
Pizza and Taco's Party Plans
What we need
1. Banner
PARTY!
2. Punch
3. Cups
4. Balloons
WHERE
THE WATER PARK!!!
Guest List
1. Cake
2. Ice Cream
3 and 4. The Chicken Tender twins
5. Hamburger
6. Hot Dog
7. Cheeseburger
Invitation time! I have paper.
I still have my pen!

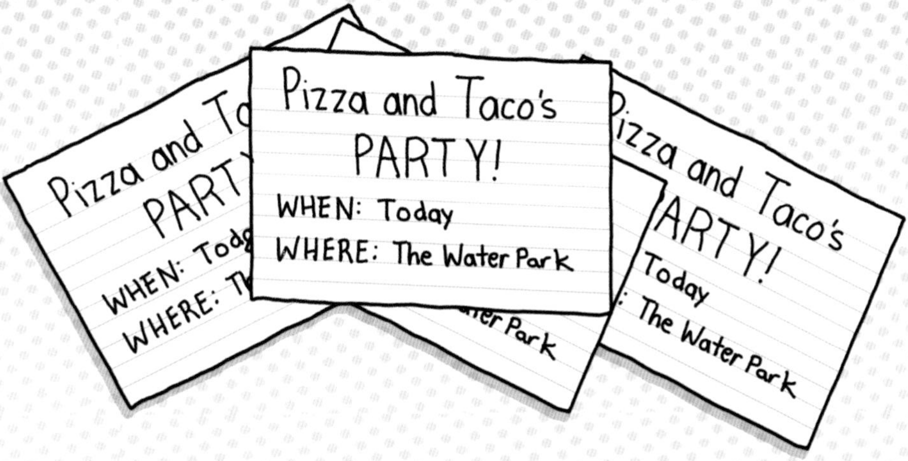
Pizza and Taco's
PARTY!
WHEN: Today
WHERE: The Water Park

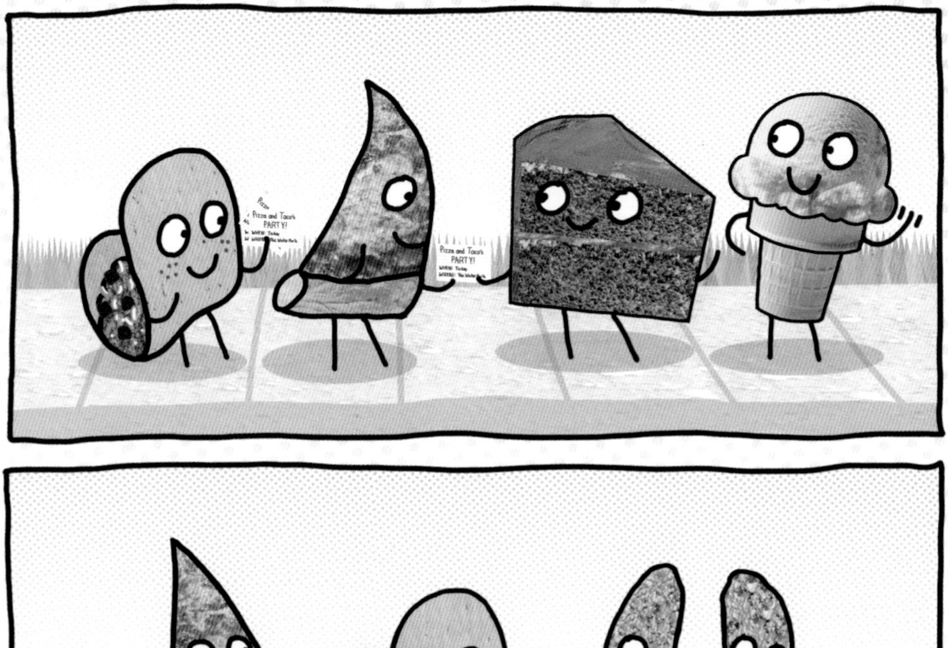

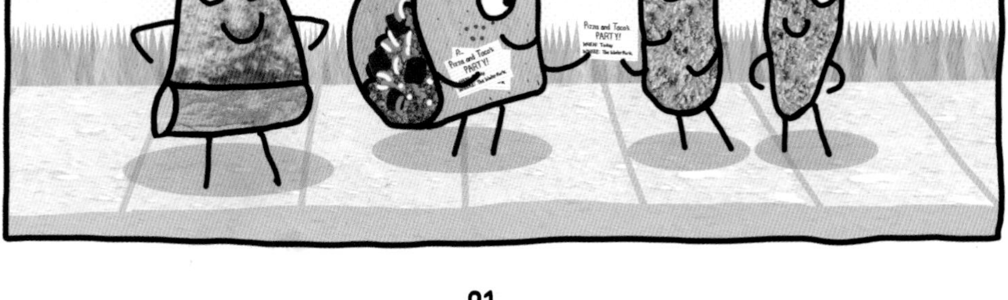

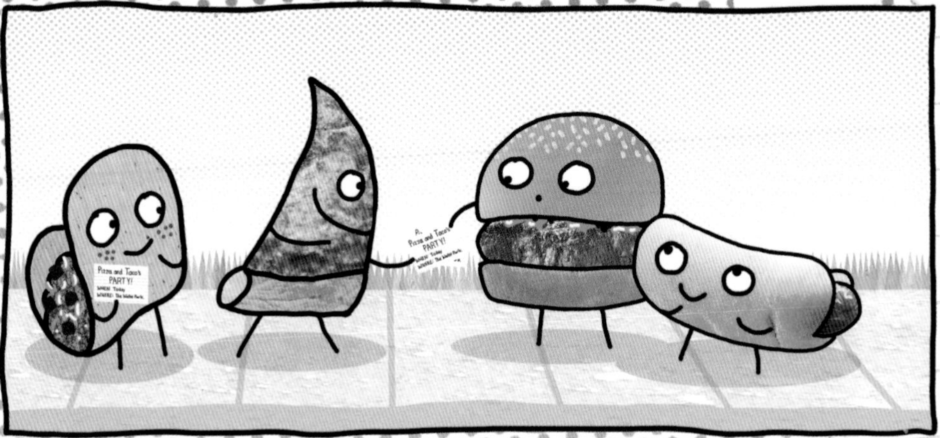
Pizza and Taco's
PARTY!

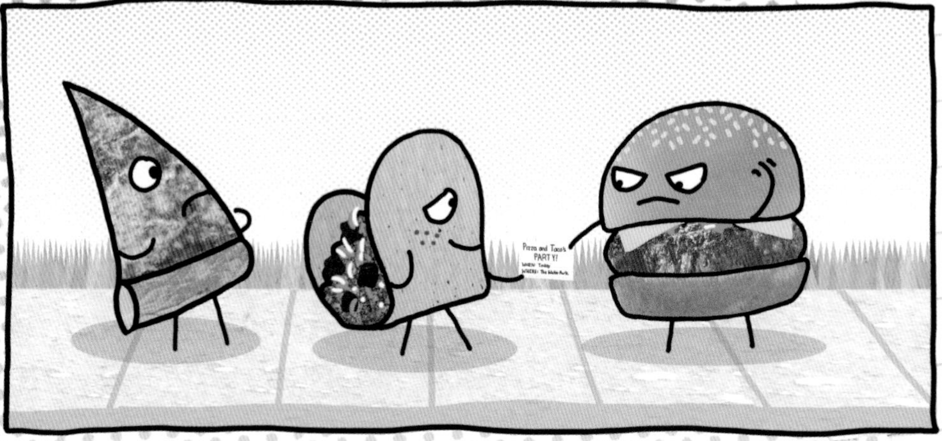
Pizza and Taco's
PARTY!

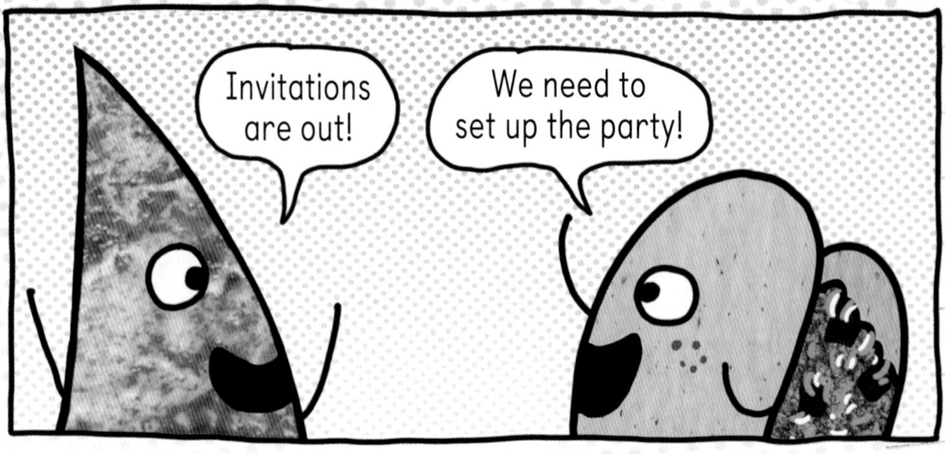
Invitations are out!
We need to set up the party!

Chapter 3
Pizza and Taco Set Up the Party

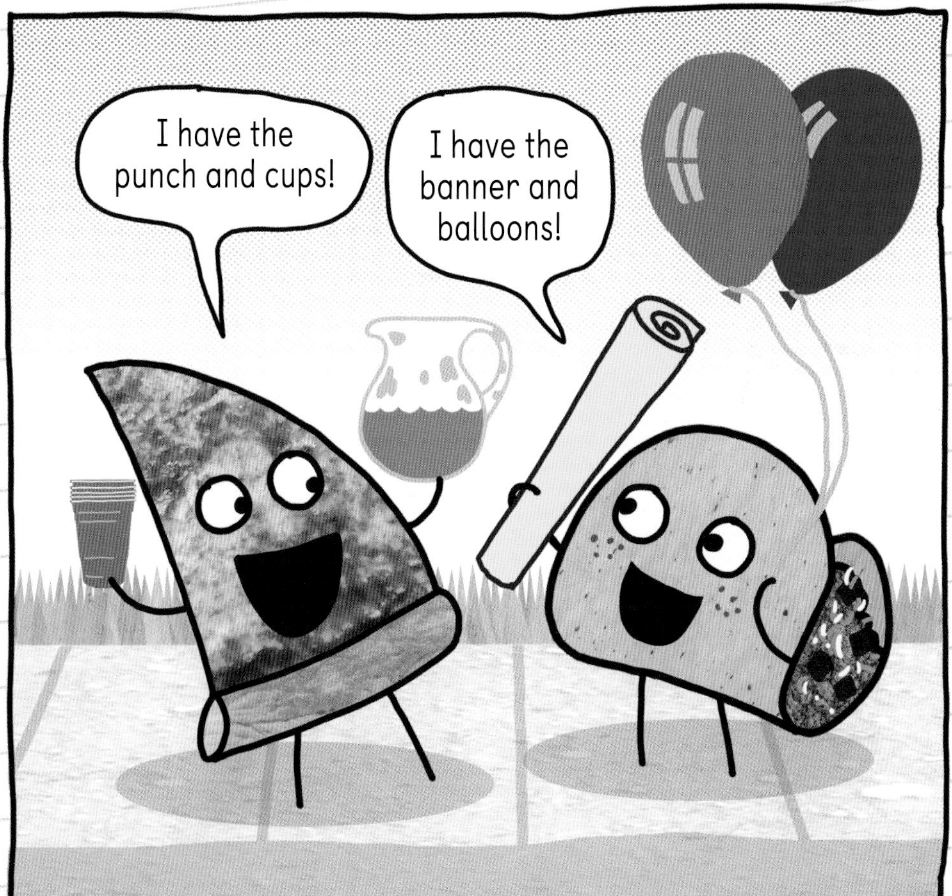
I have the punch and cups!
I have the banner and balloons!

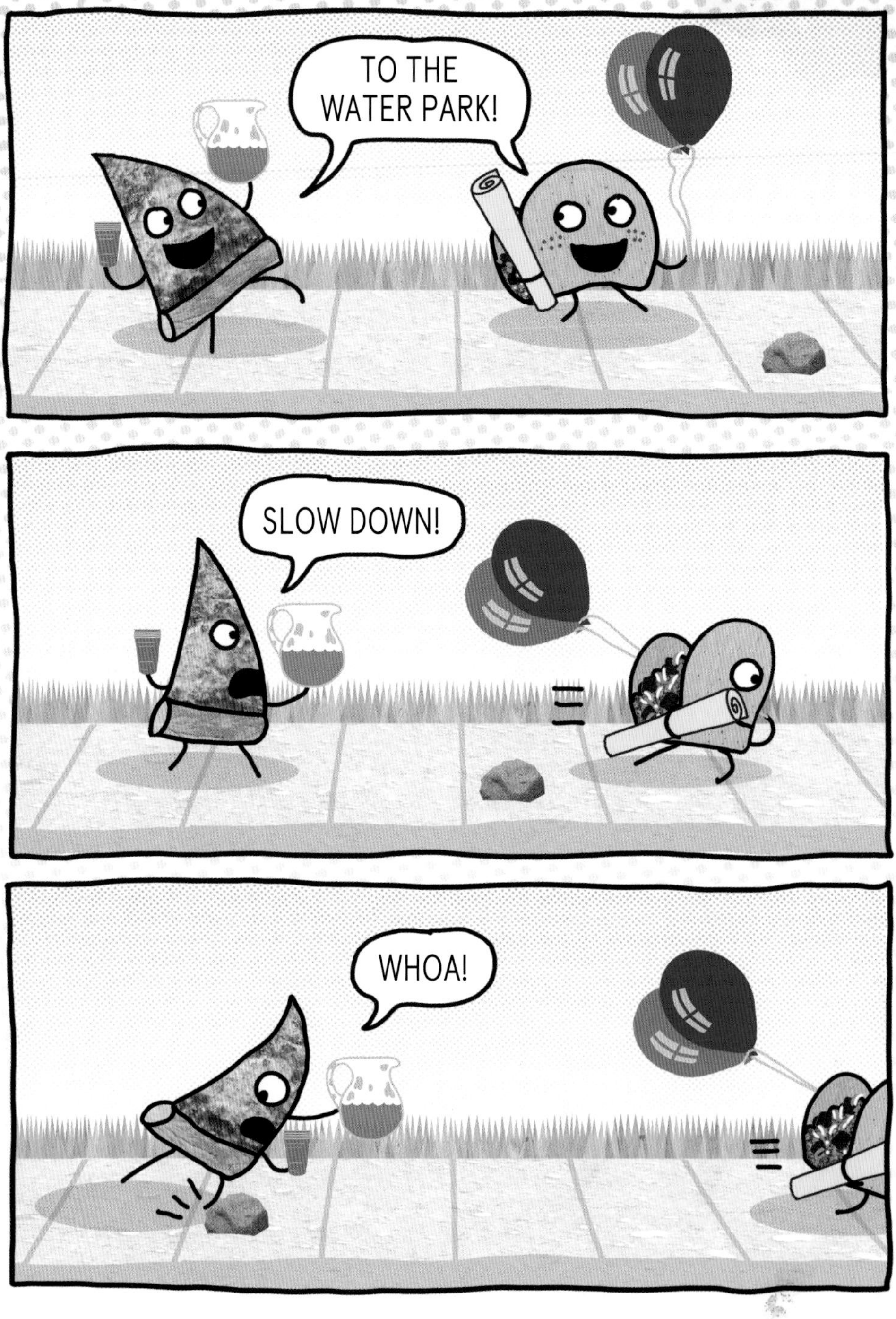
TO THE WATER PARK!
SLOW DOWN!
WHOA!

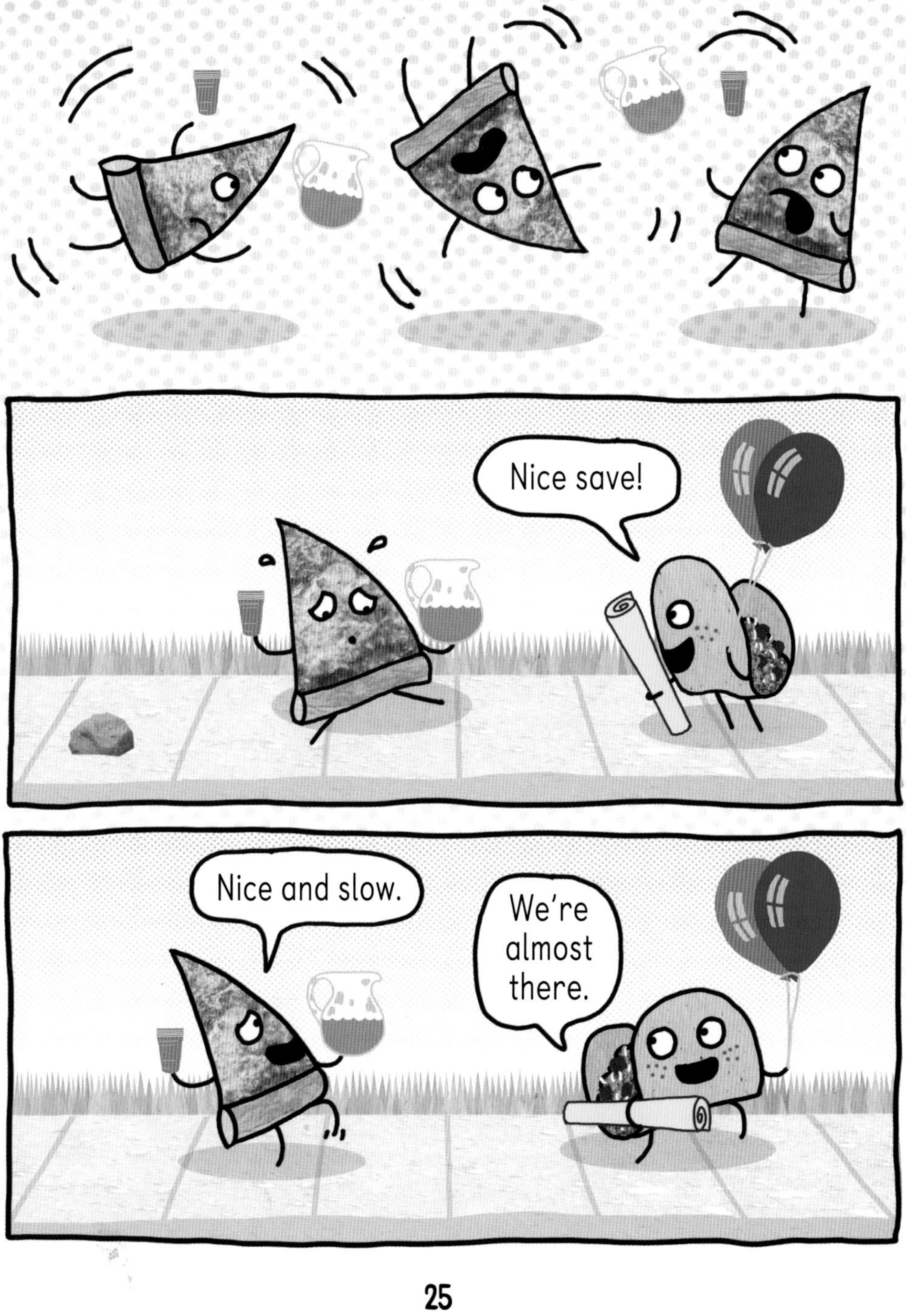
Nice save!
Nice and slow.
We're almost there.

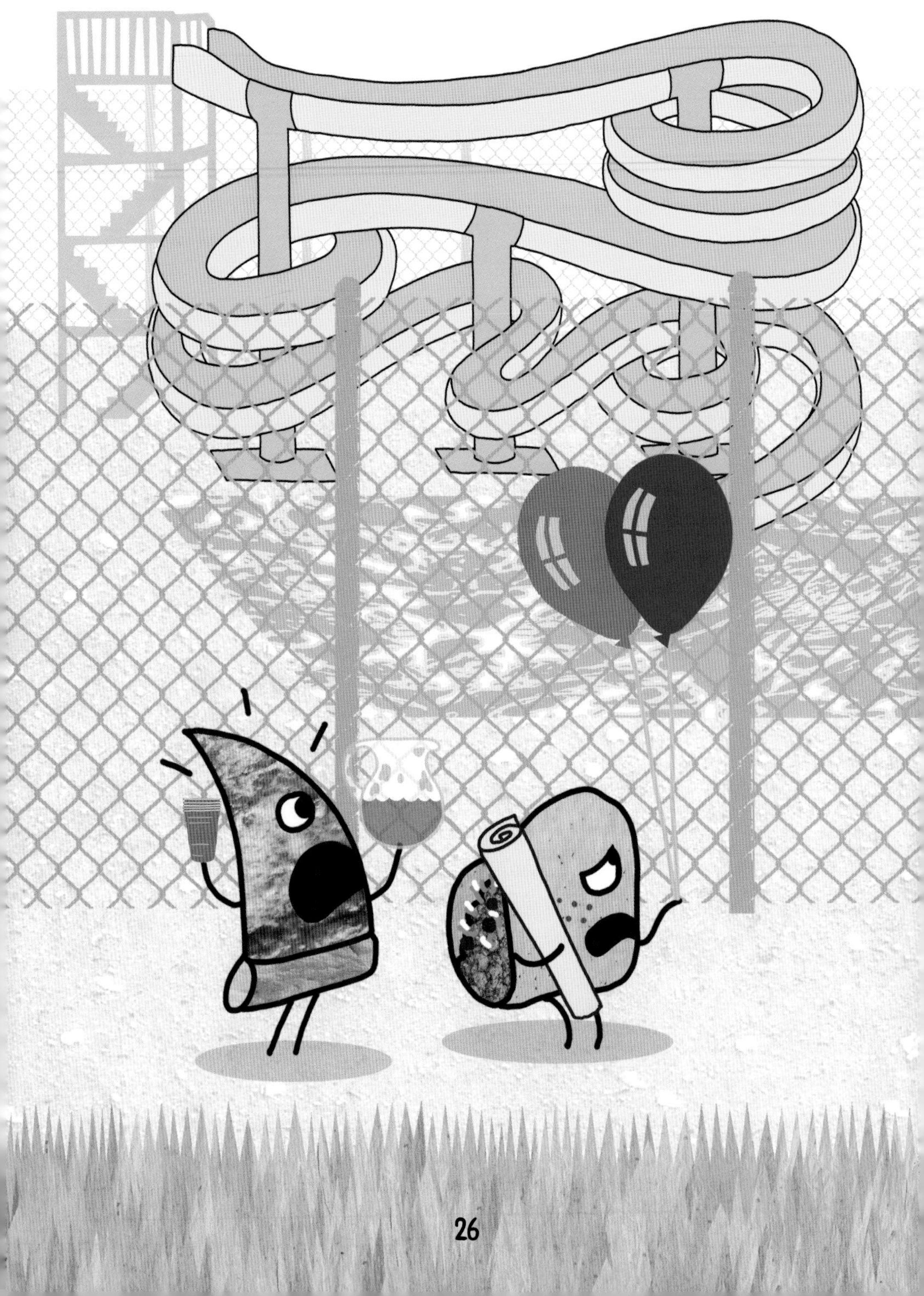

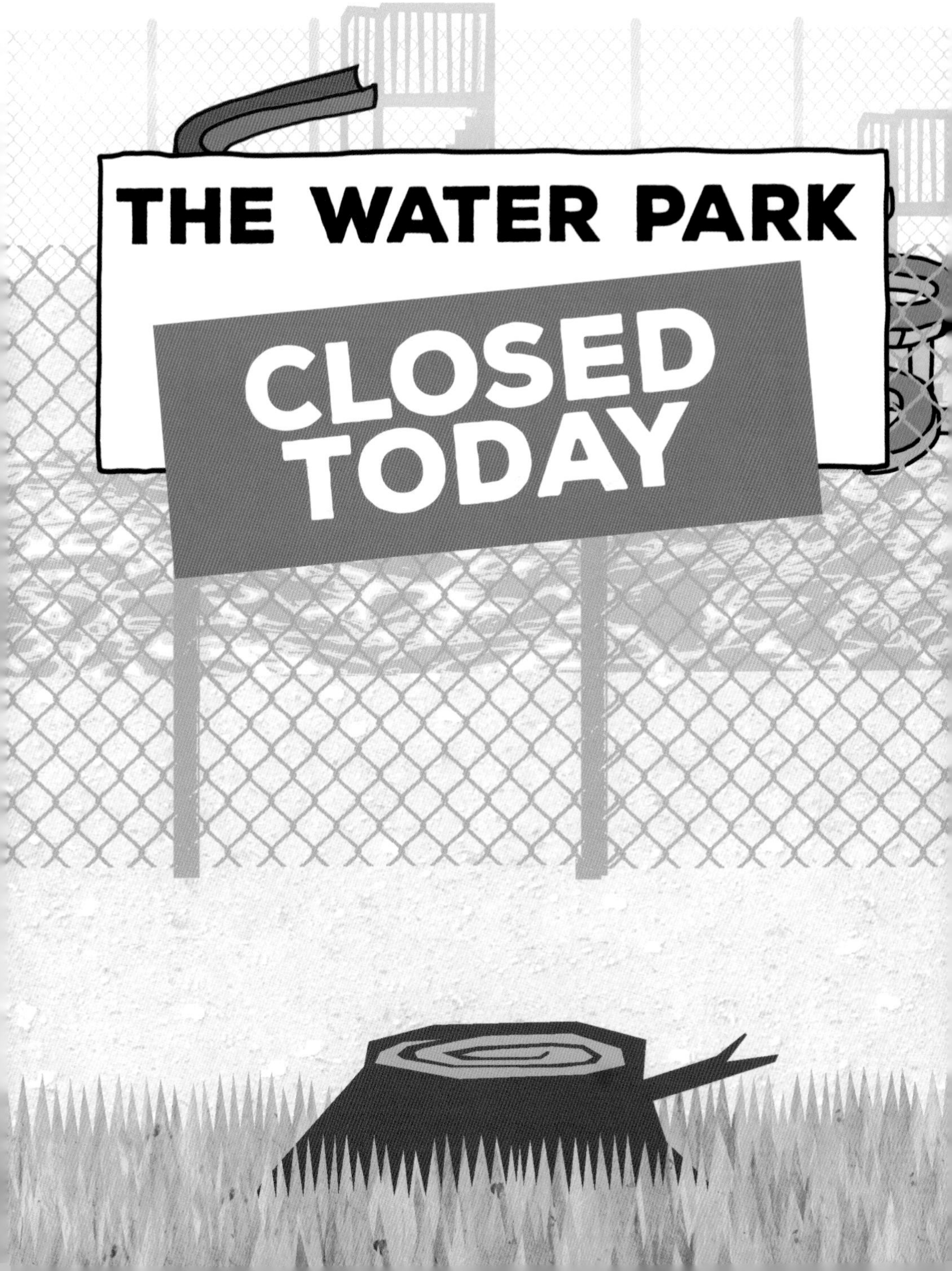
THE WATER PARK
CLOSED TODAY

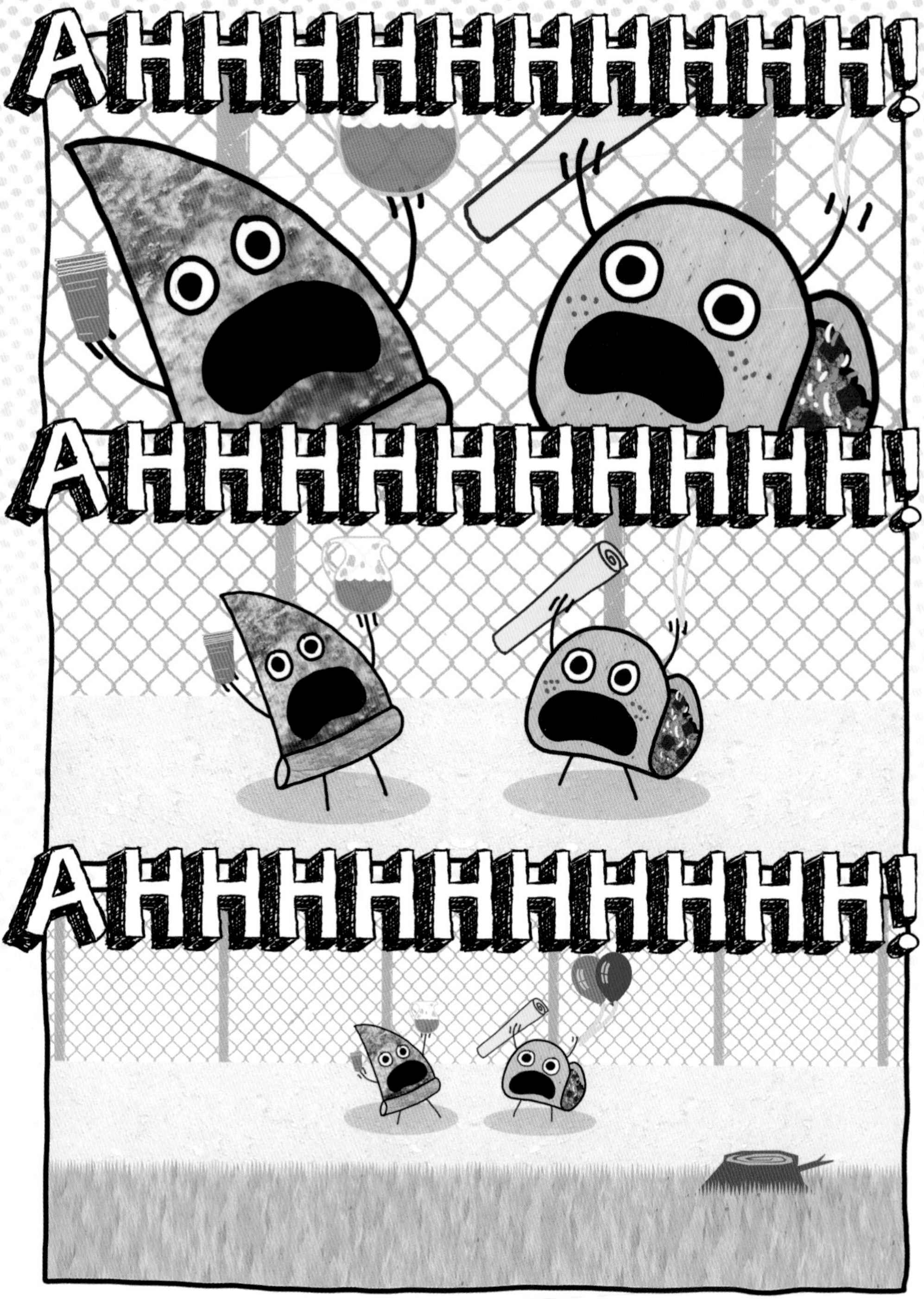
AHHHHHHHHHHHH!
AHHHHHHHHHHHH!
AHHHHHHHHHHHH!

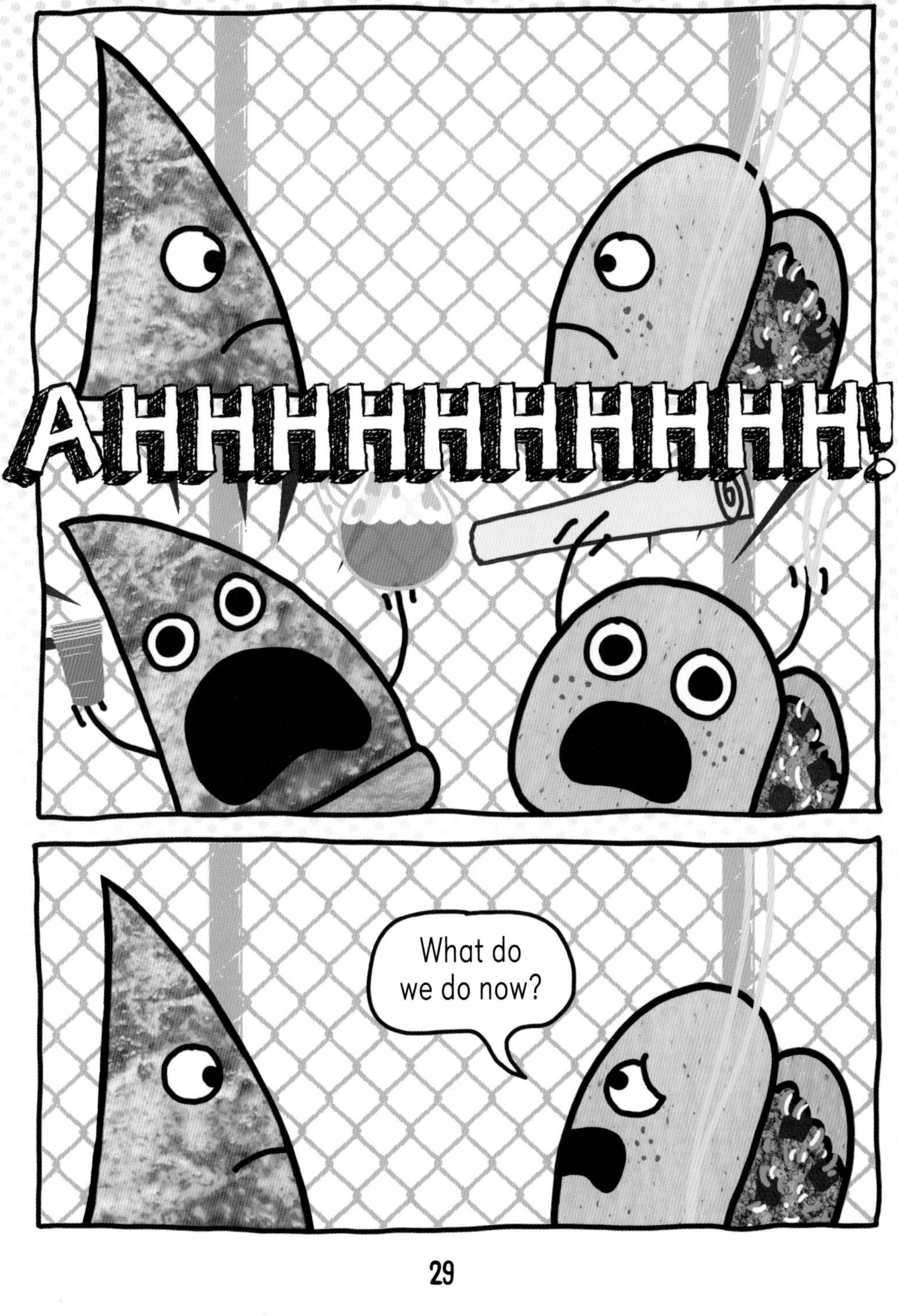
AHHHHHHHHHHHH!
What do we do now?

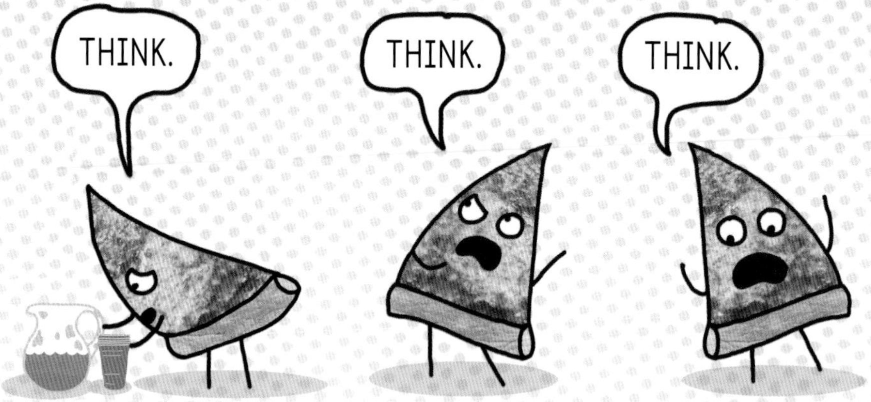
THINK.
THINK.
THINK.

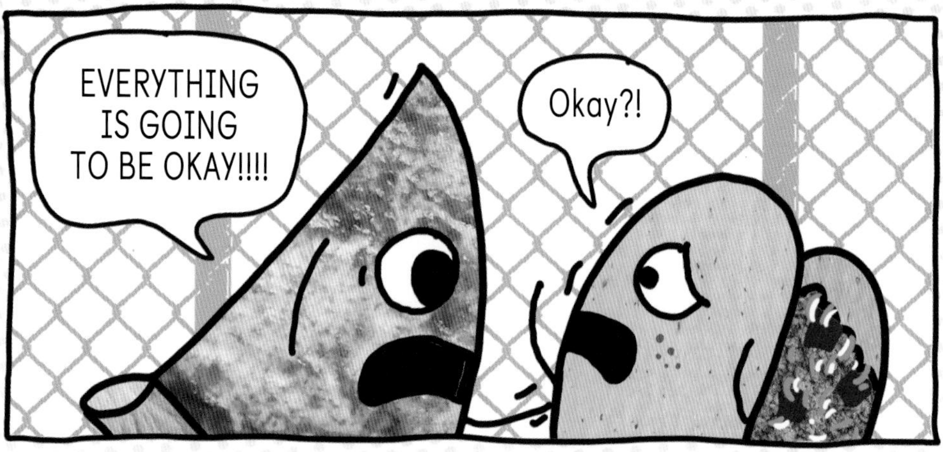
EVERYTHING IS GOING TO BE OKAY!!!!
Okay?!

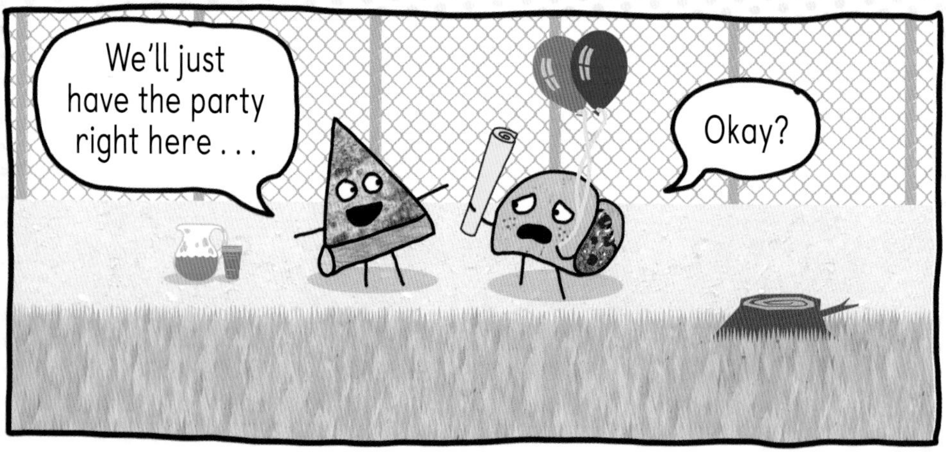
We'll just have the party right here . . .
Okay?

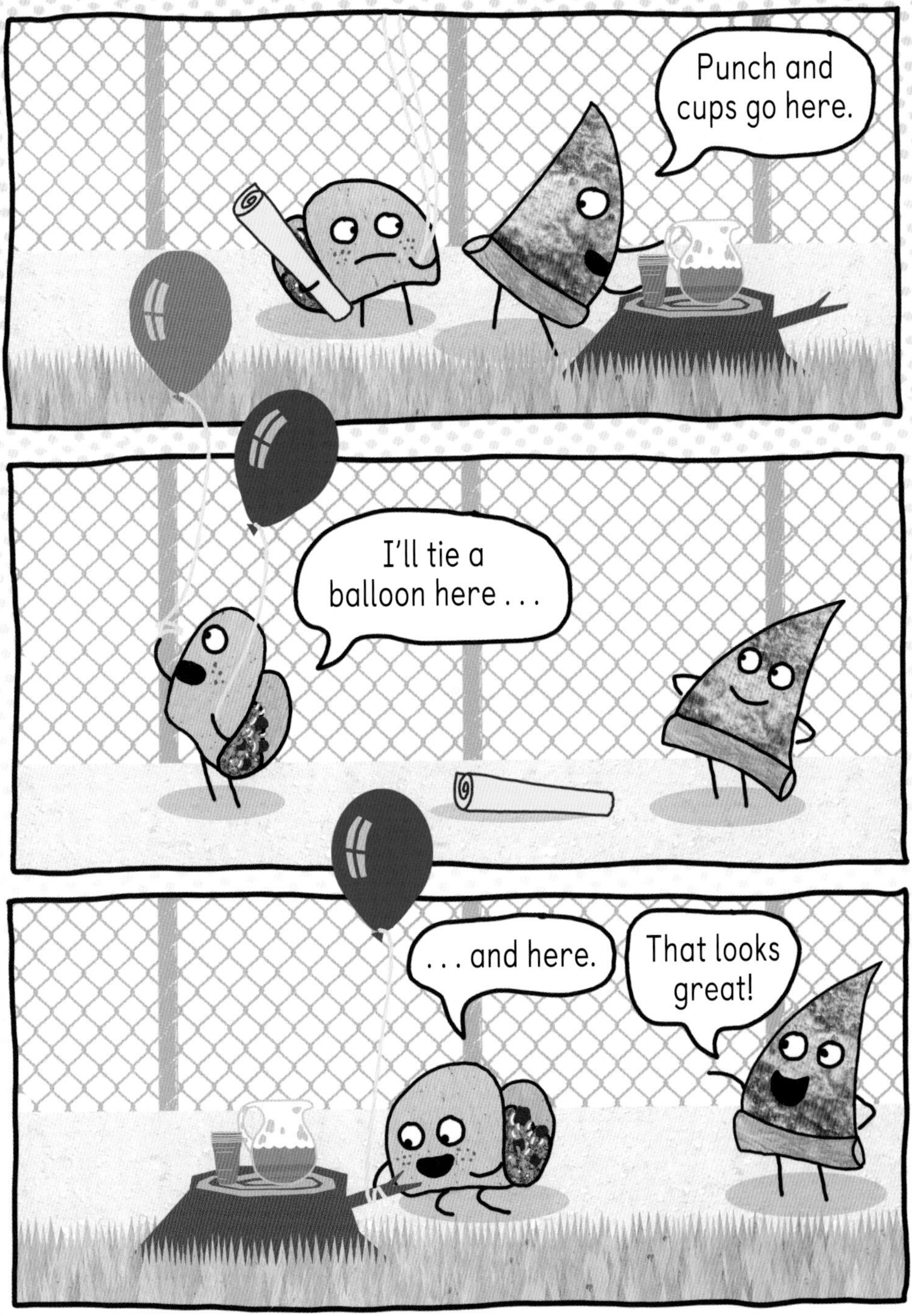
Punch and cups go here.
I'll tie a balloon here . . .
. . . and here.
That looks great!

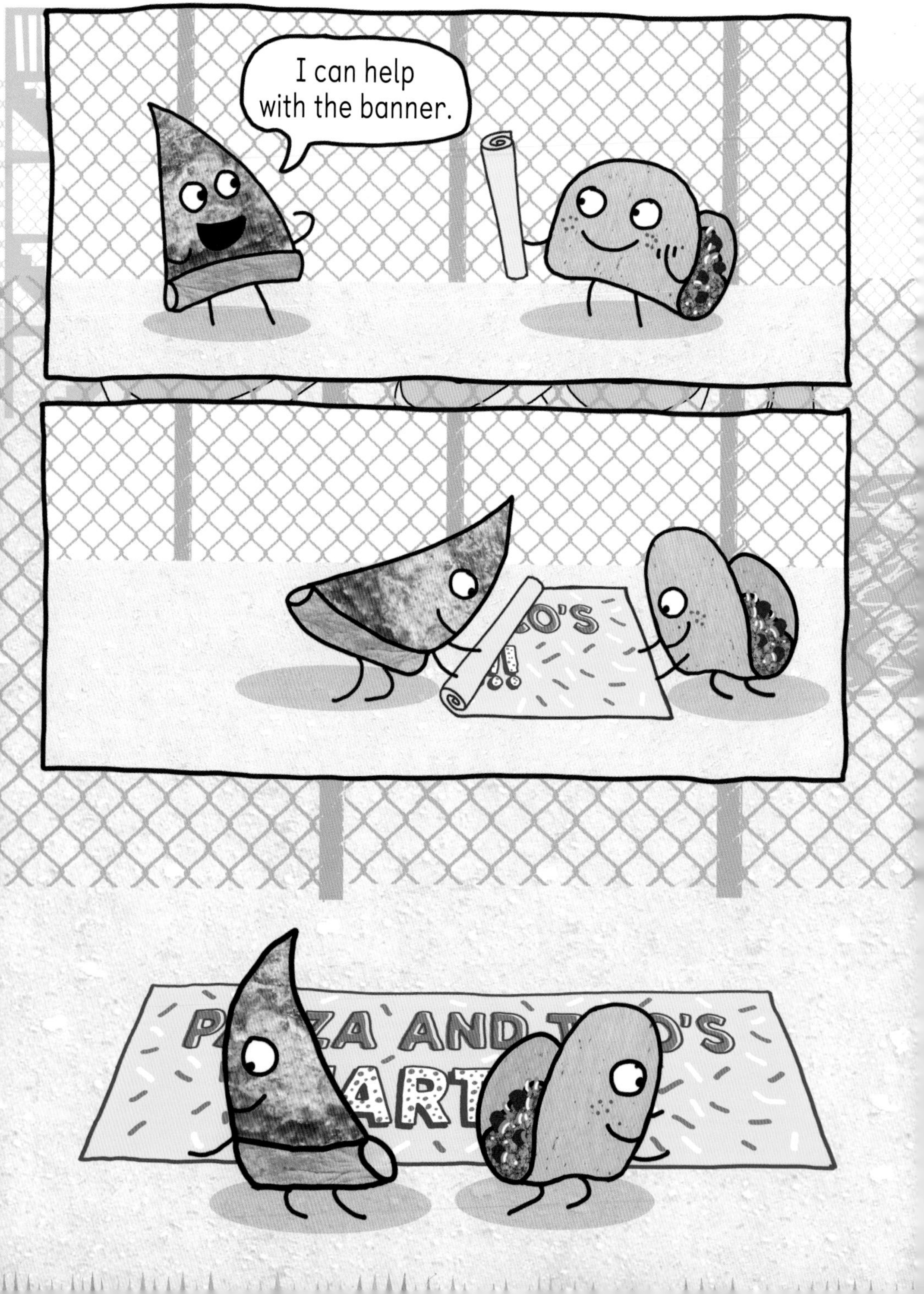
I can help with the banner.

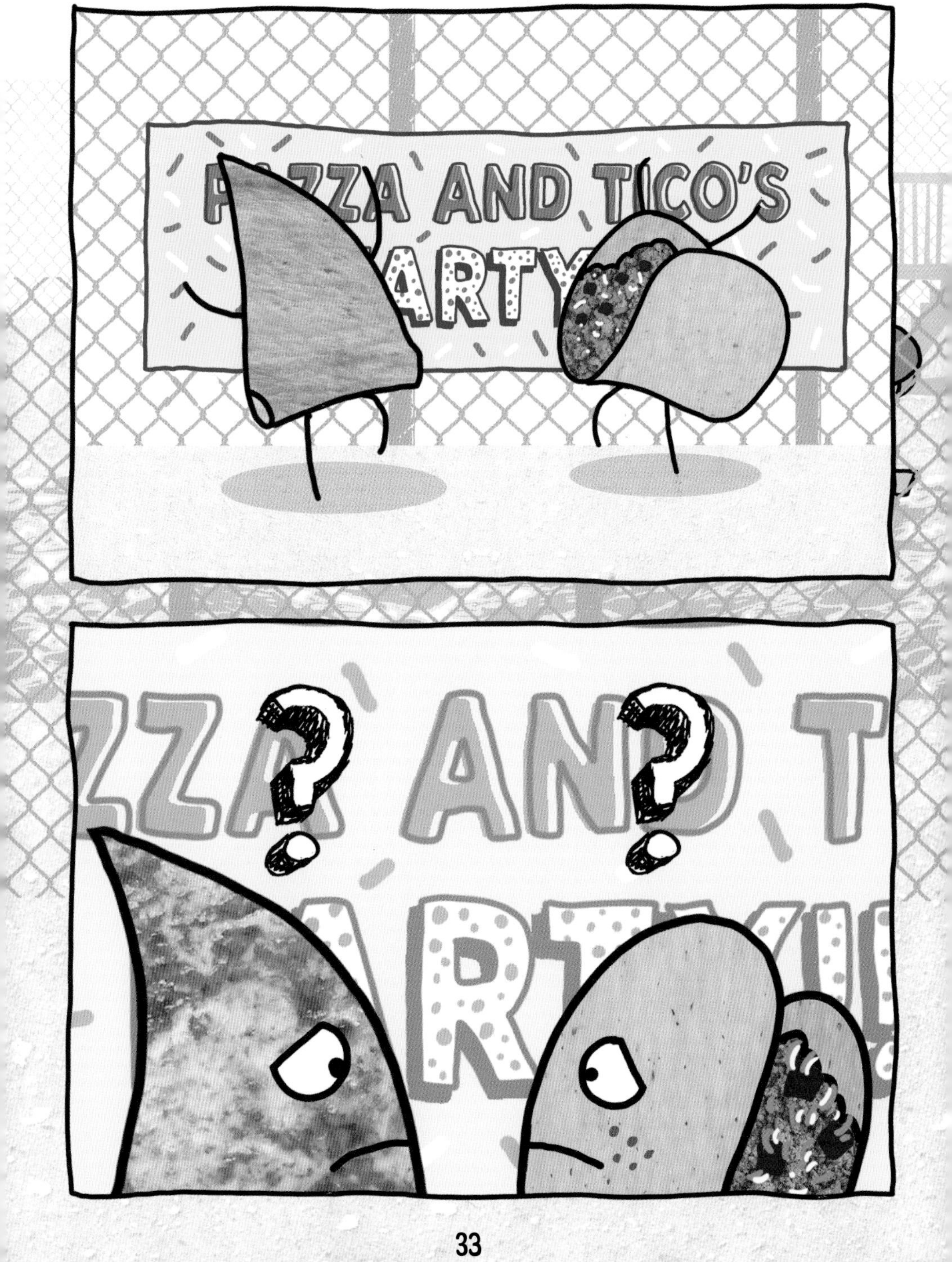
ZZA AND
ARTY
?
?

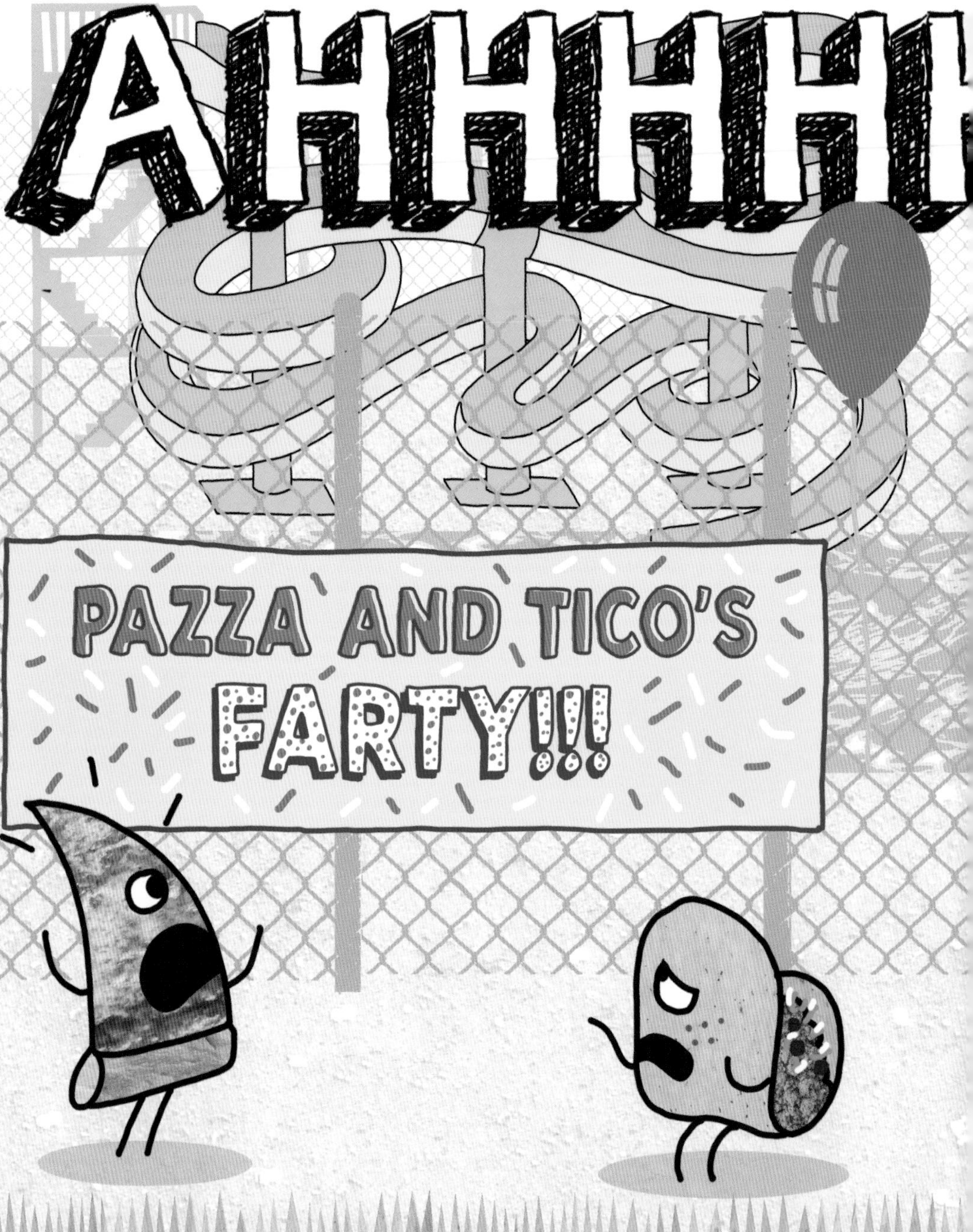
AHHHHH
PAZZA AND TICO'S
FARTY!!!

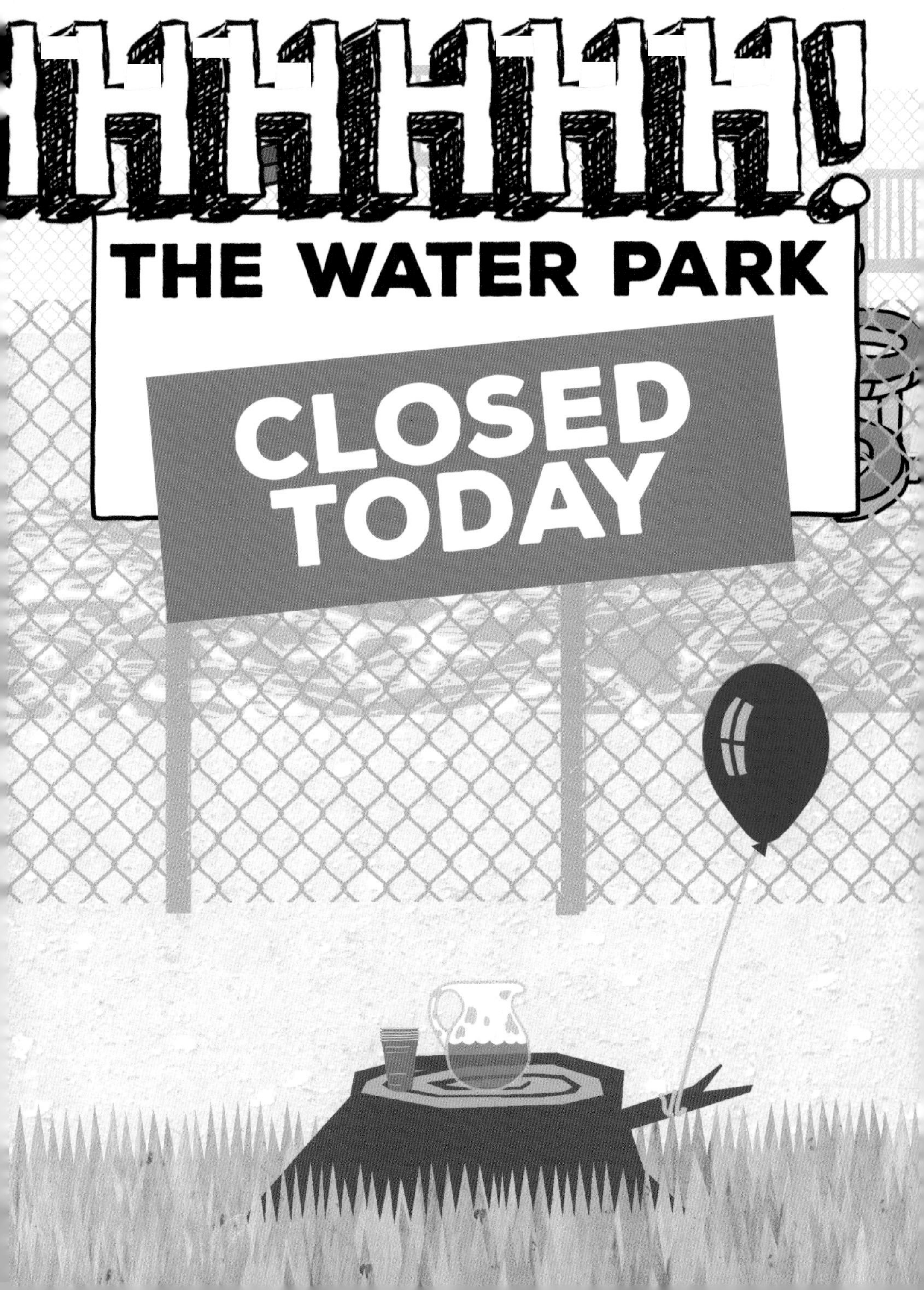
THE WATER PARK
CLOSED TODAY

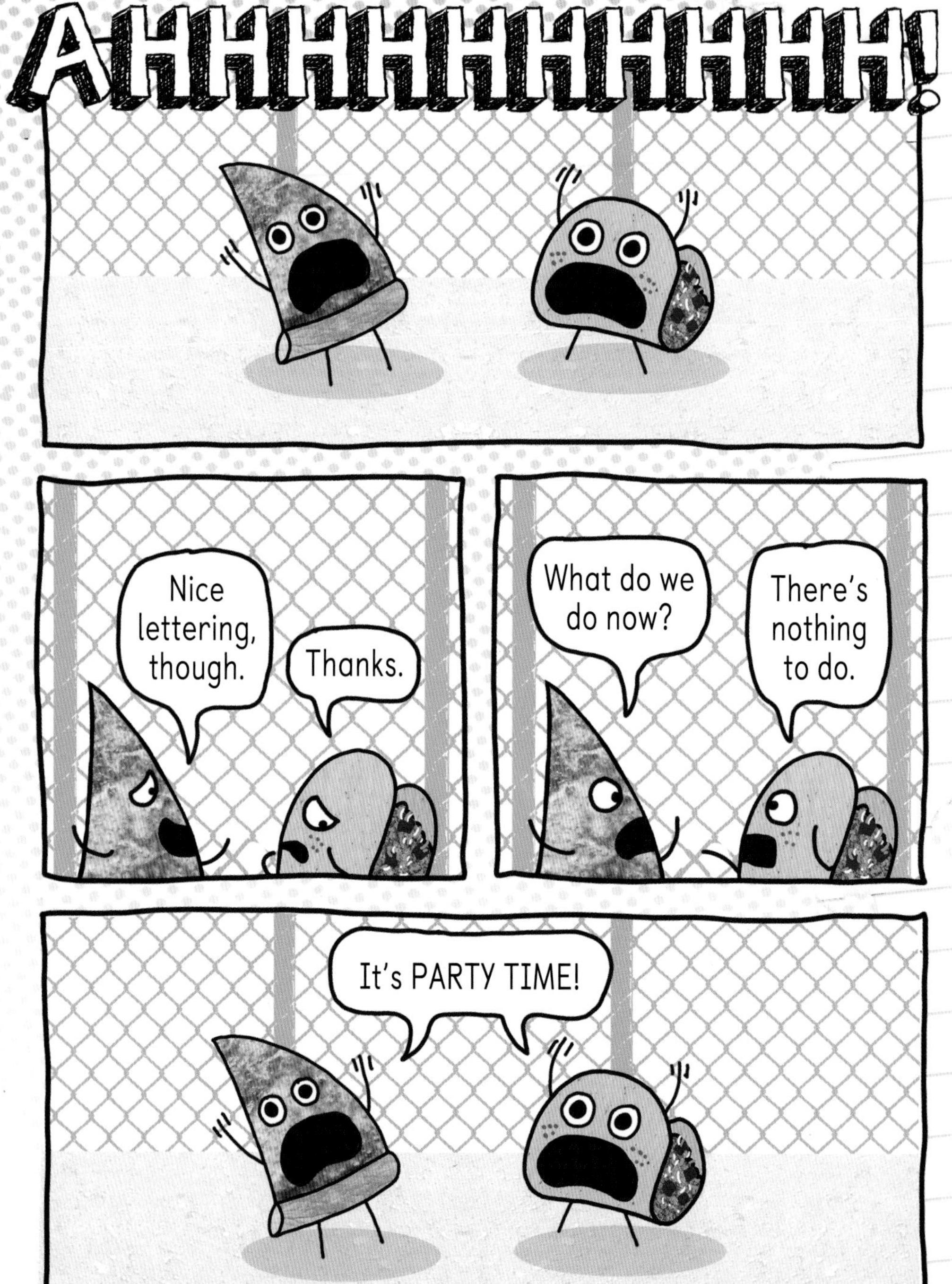
AHHHHHHHHHHHHH!
Nice lettering, though.
Thanks.
What do we do now?
There's nothing to do.
It's PARTY TIME!

Chapter 4
PARTY TIME!

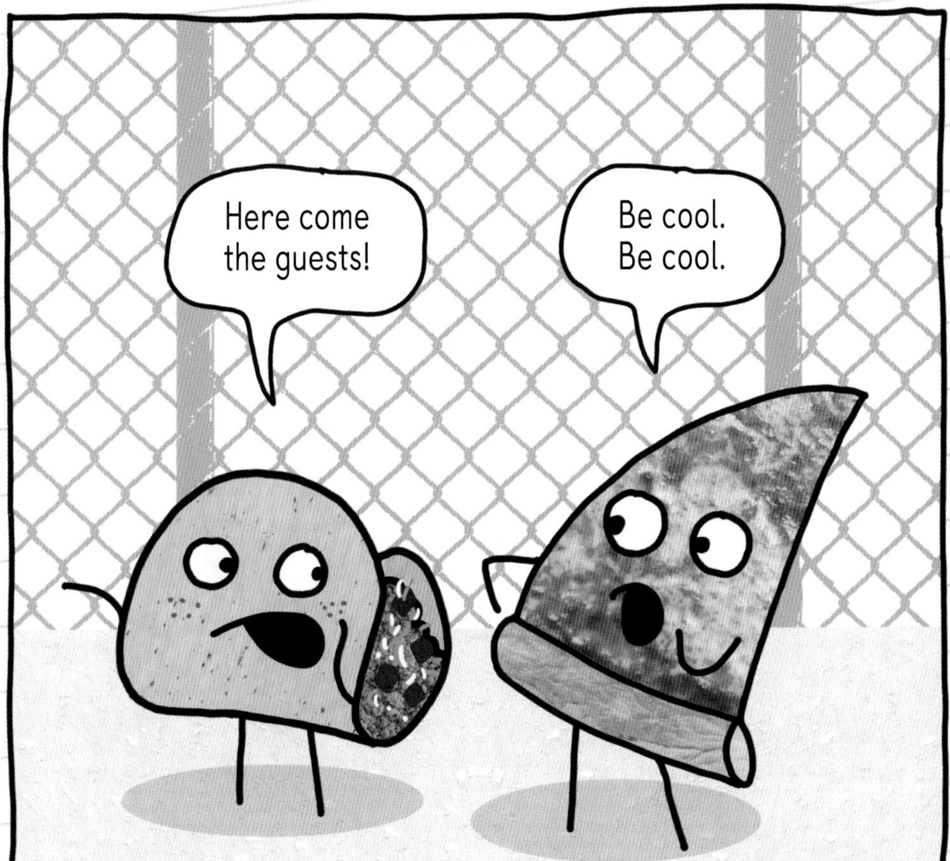
Here come the guests!
Be cool. Be cool.

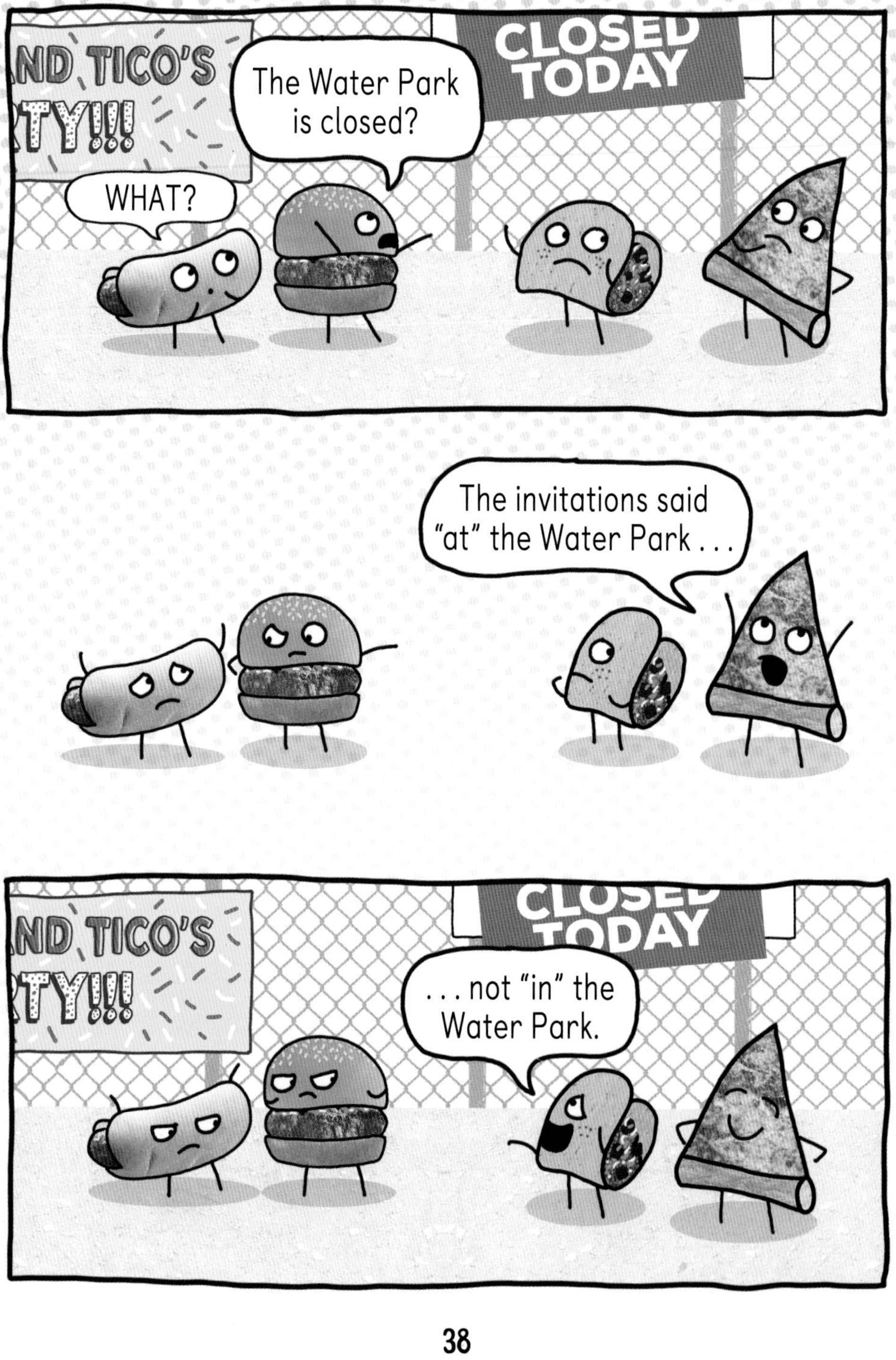
ND TICO'S
CLOSED TODAY
The Water Park is closed?
WHAT?
The invitations said "at" the Water Park . . .
ND TICO'S
TODAY
. . . not "in" the Water Park.

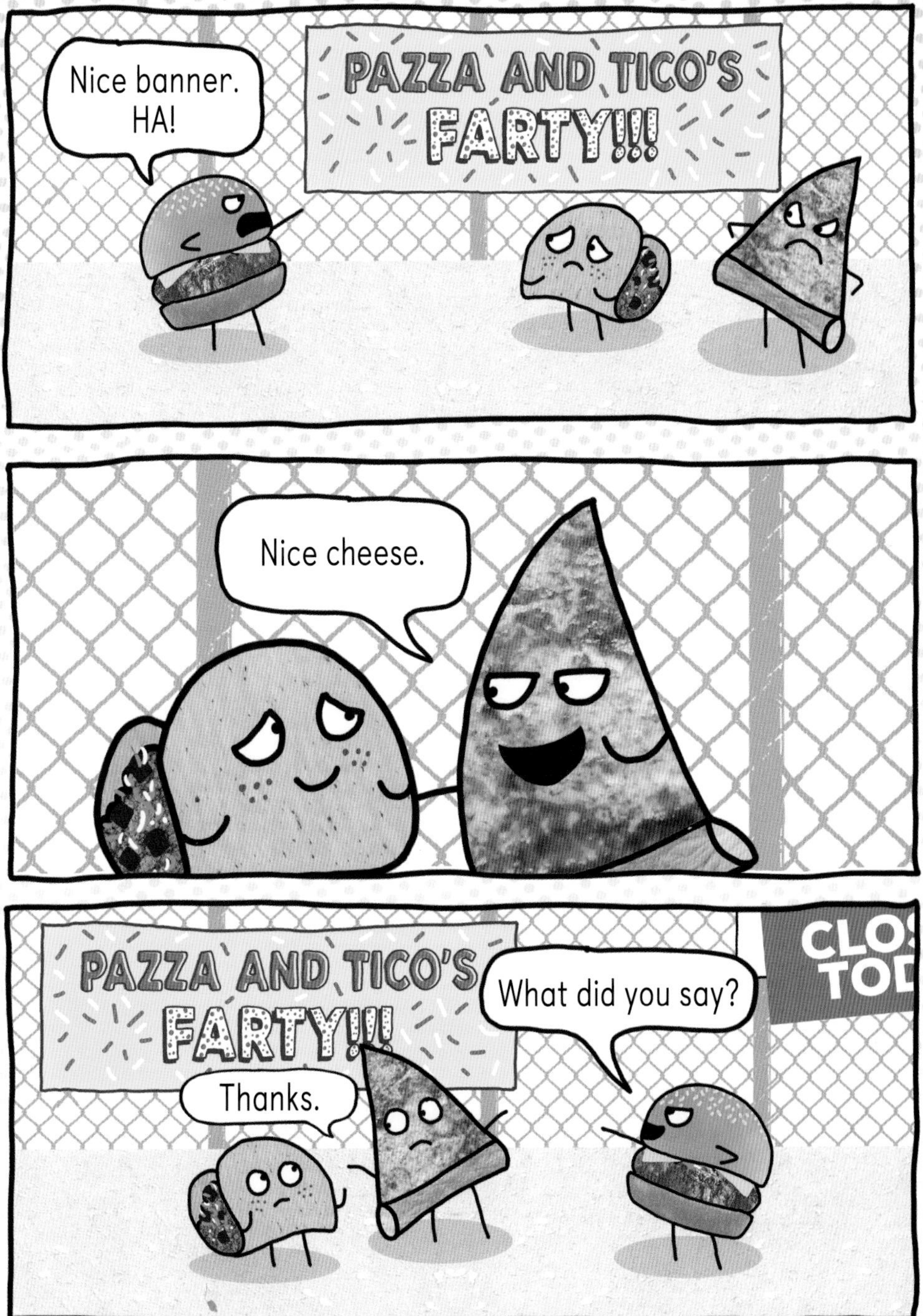
Nice banner.
HA!
PAZZA AND TICO'S
FARTY!!!
Nice cheese.
PAZZA AND TICO'S
FARTY!!!
What did you say?
Thanks.

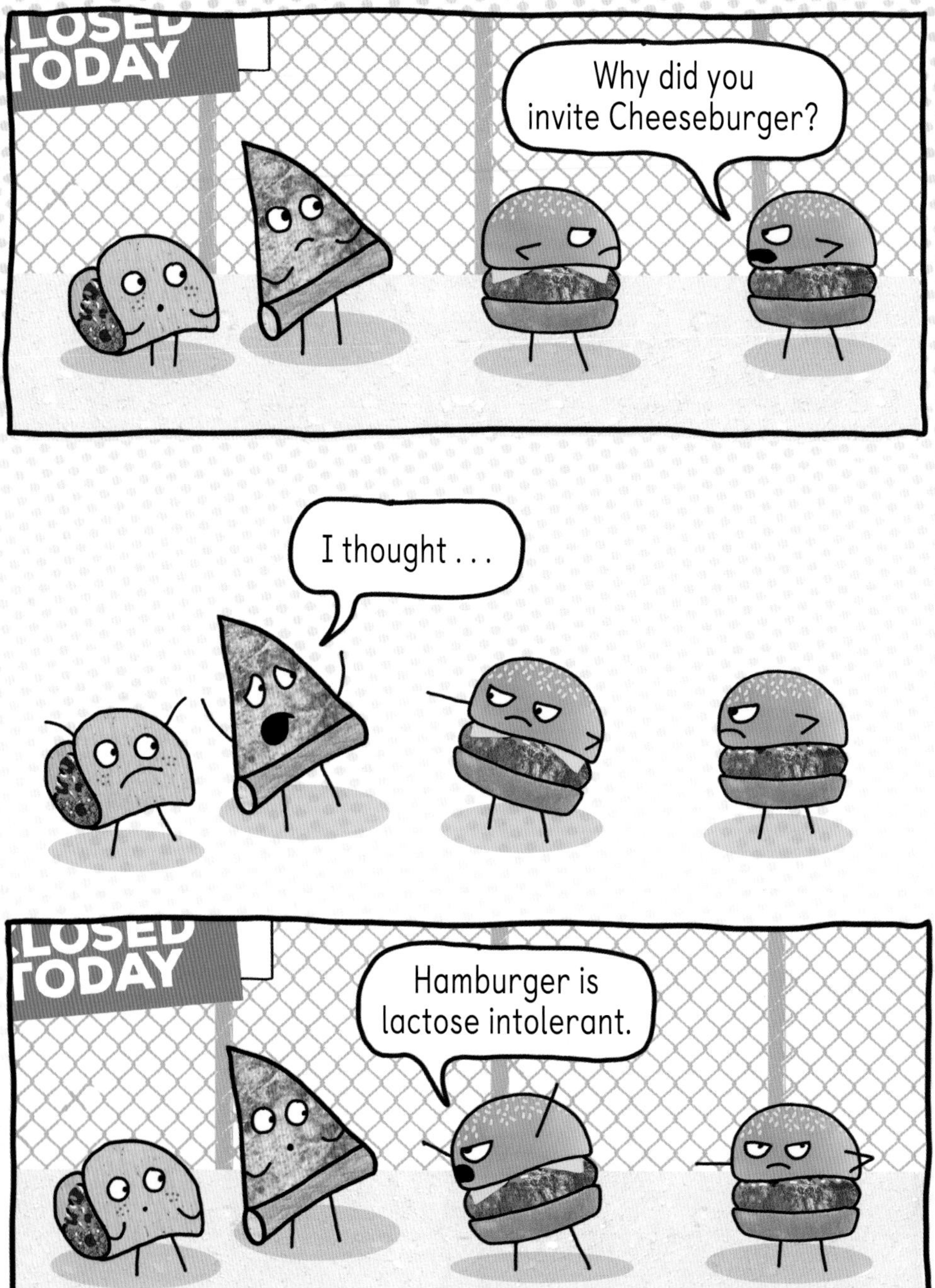

LOSED
TODAY
Why did you invite Cheeseburger?
I thought . . .
LOSED
TODAY
Hamburger is lactose intolerant.

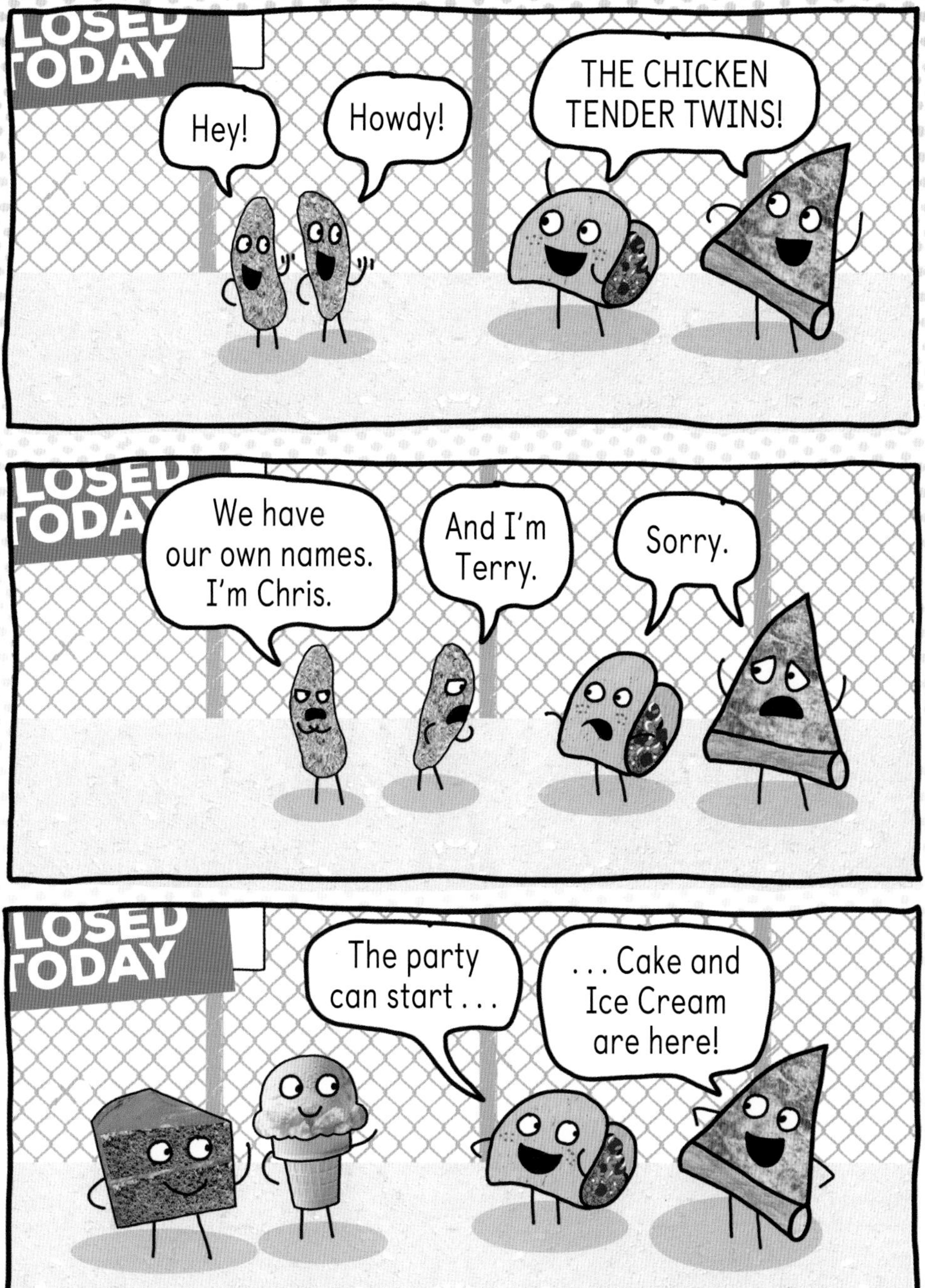
LOSED
TODAY
Hey!
Howdy!
THE CHICKEN TENDER TWINS!
LOSED
TODA
We have our own names. I'm Chris.
And I'm Terry.
Sorry.
LOSED
TODAY
The party can start . . .
. . . Cake and Ice Cream are here!

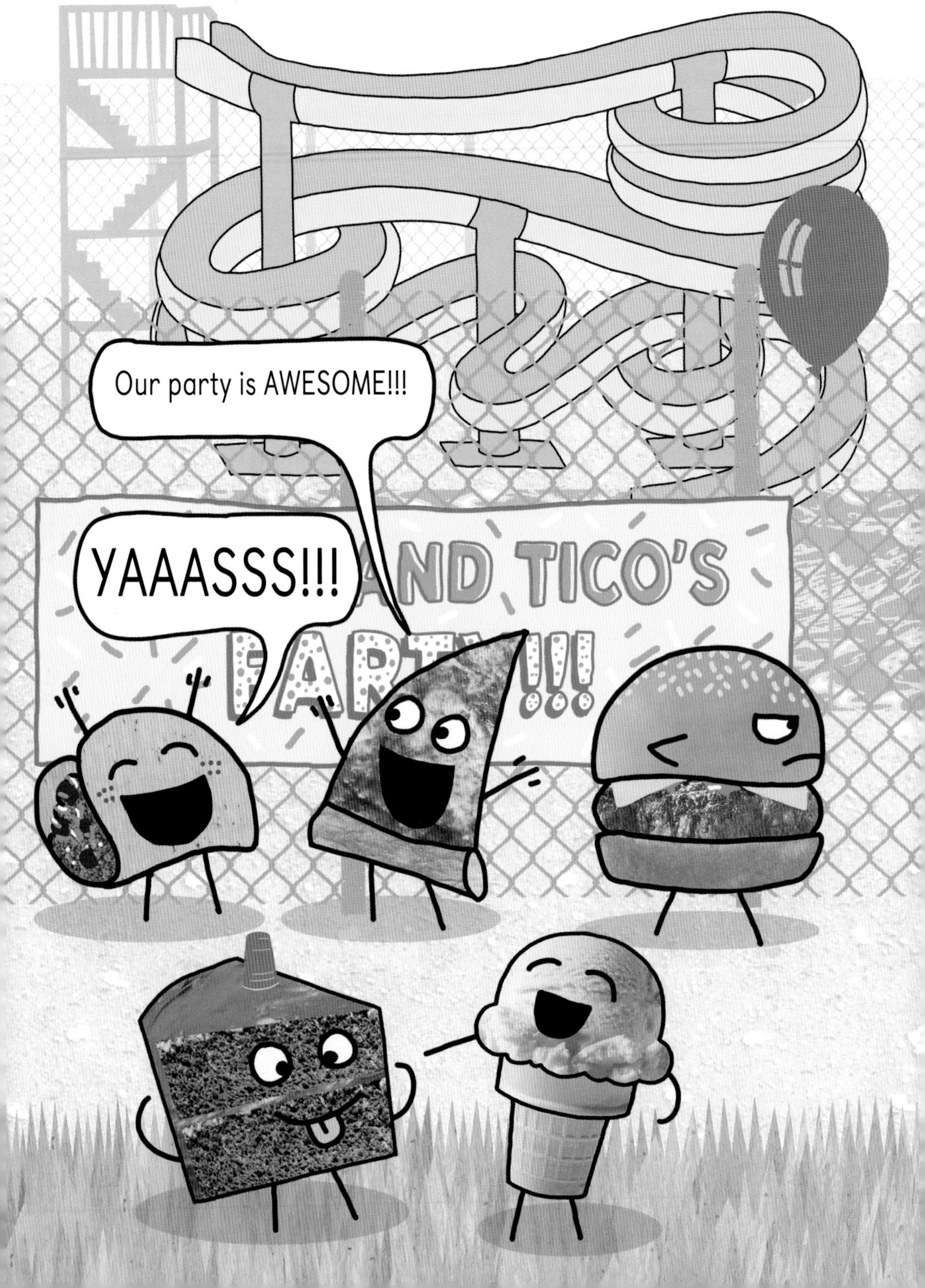
Our party is AWESOME!!!
YAAASSS!!!
AND TICO'S

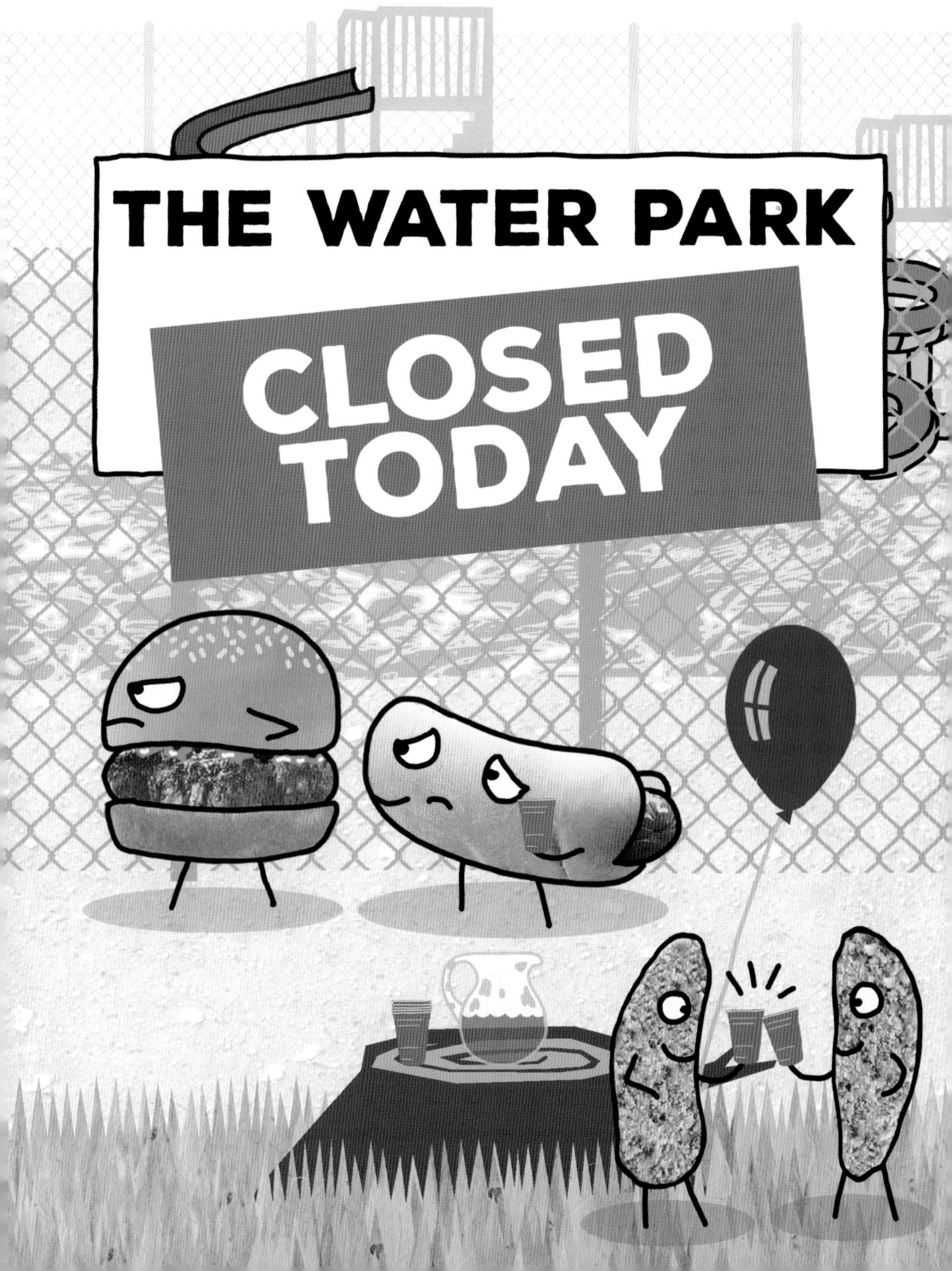
THE WATER PARK
CLOSED TODAY

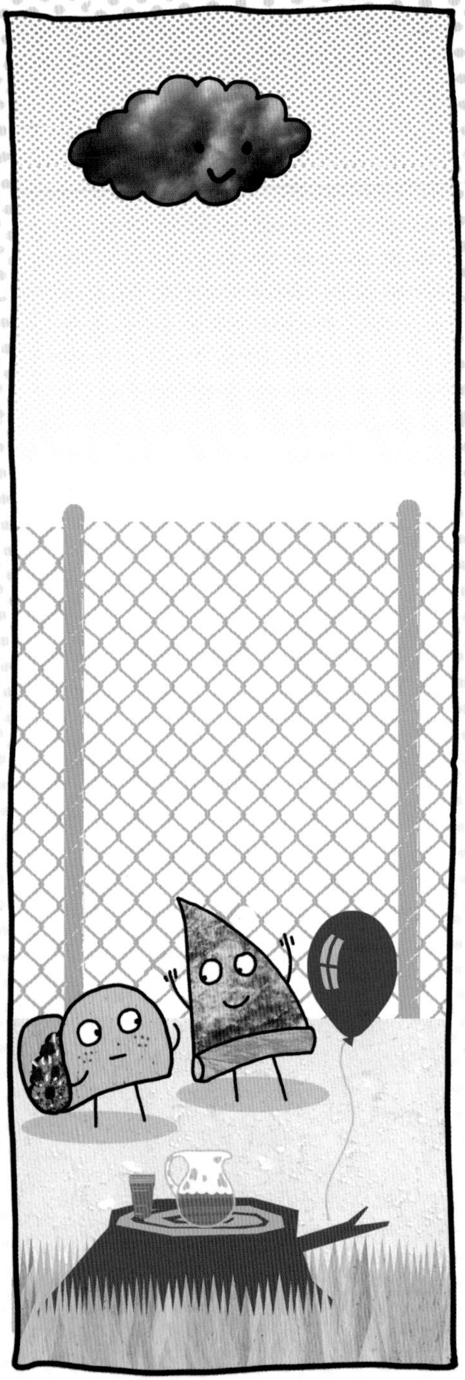

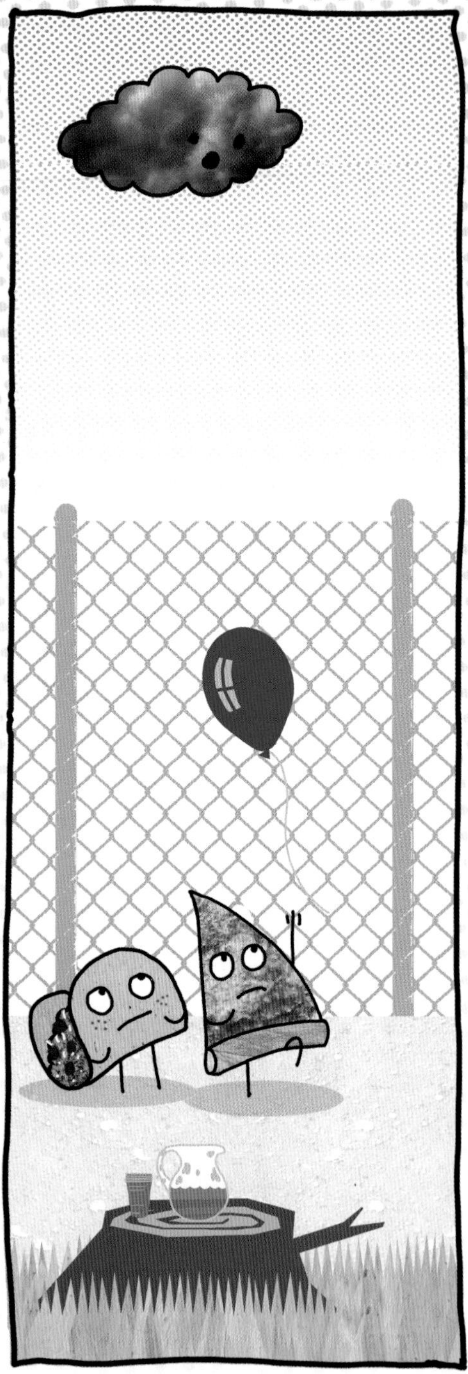

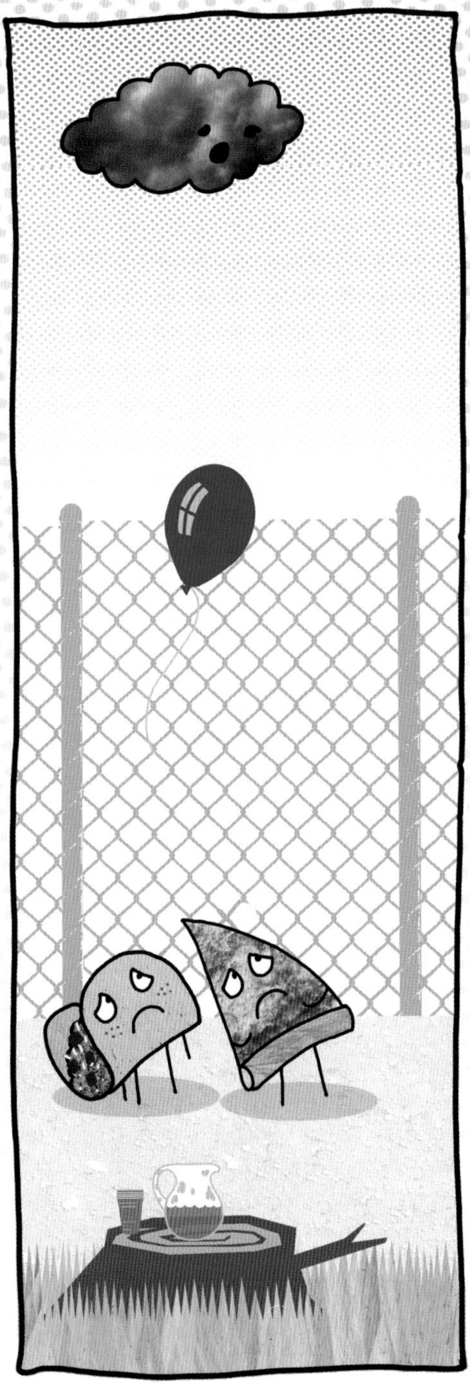

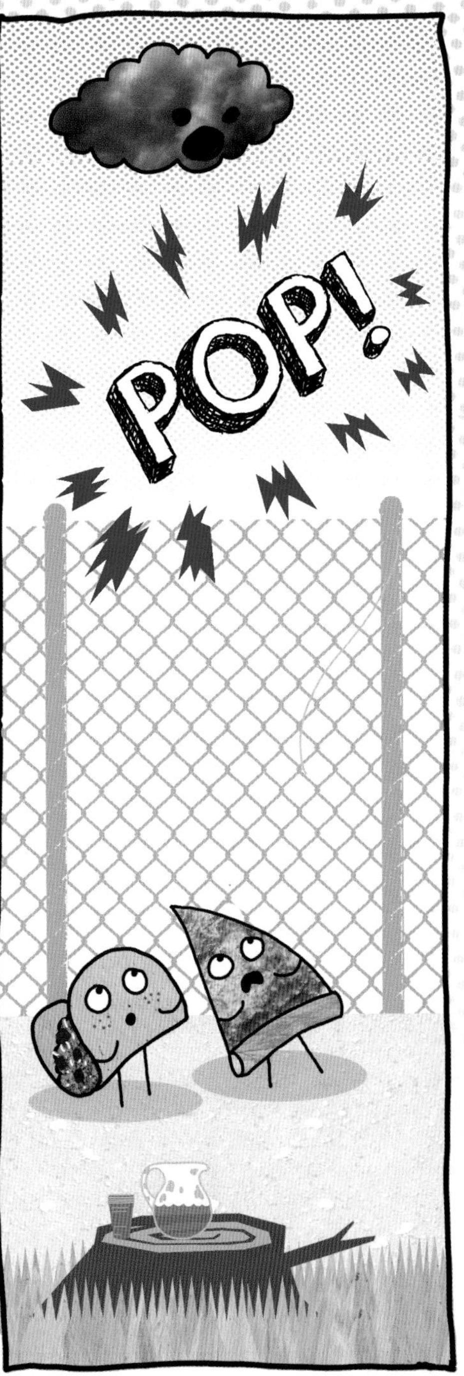
POP!

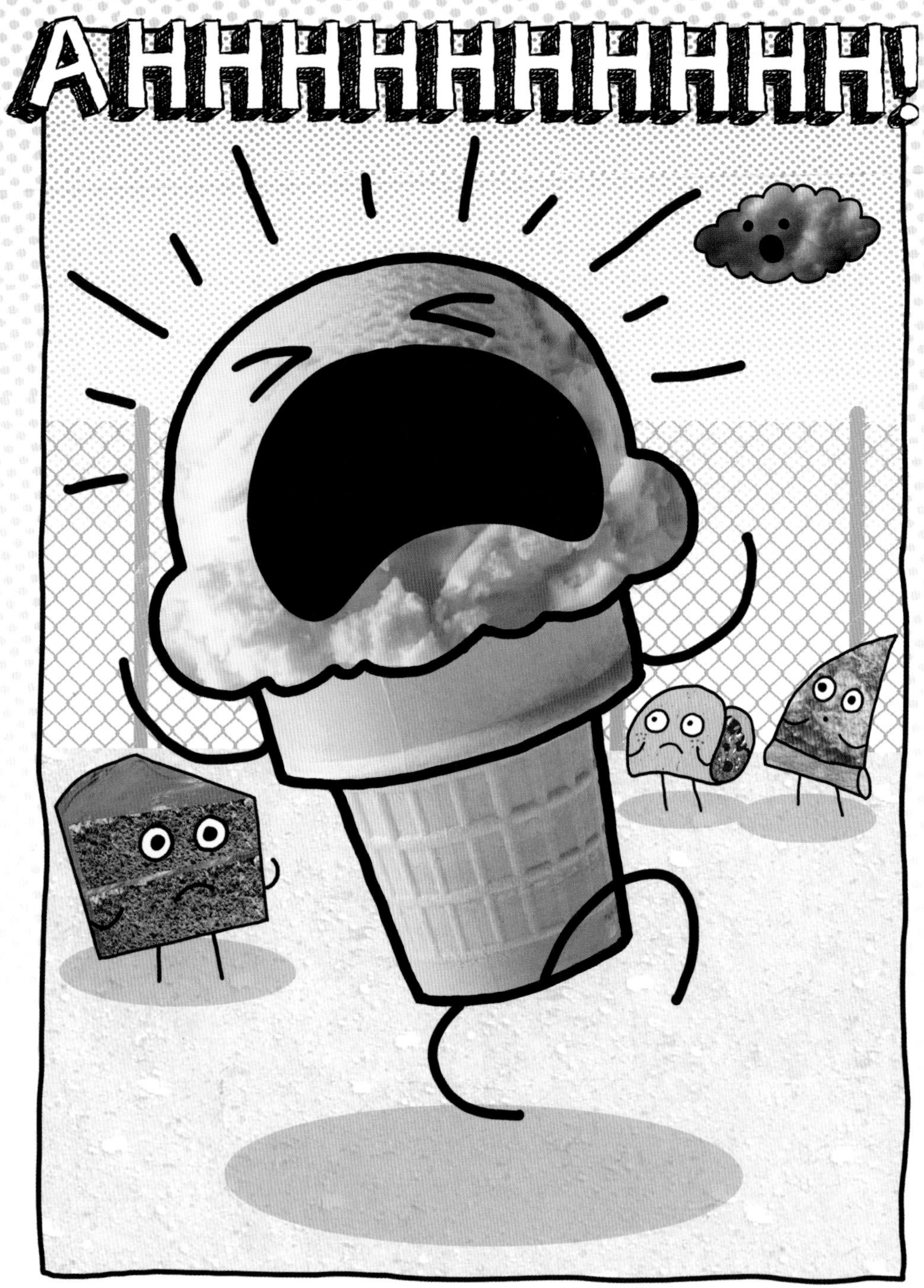
AHHHHHHHHHHHHH!

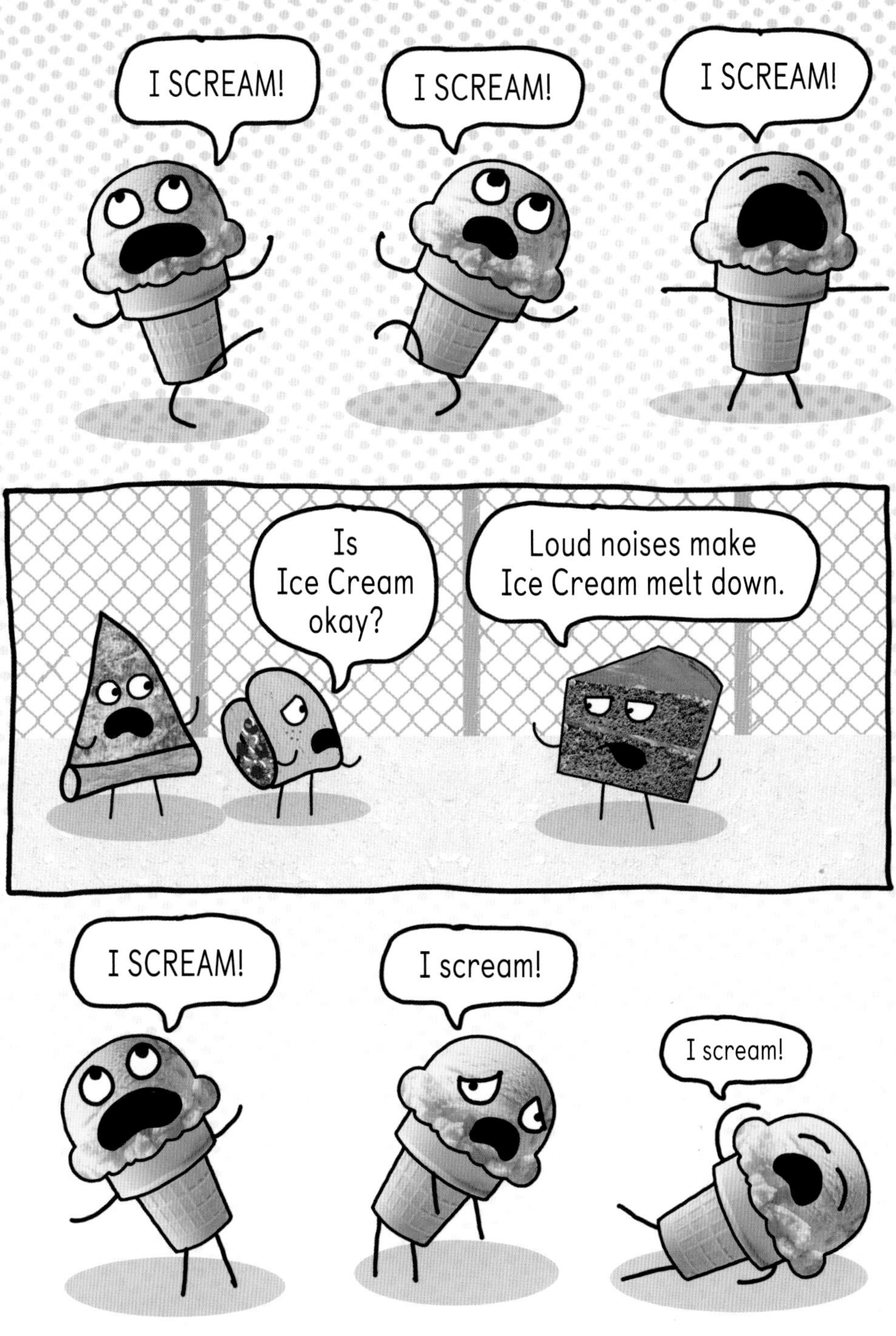
I SCREAM!
I SCREAM!
I SCREAM!
Is Ice Cream okay?
Loud noises make Ice Cream melt down.
I SCREAM!
I scream!
I scream!

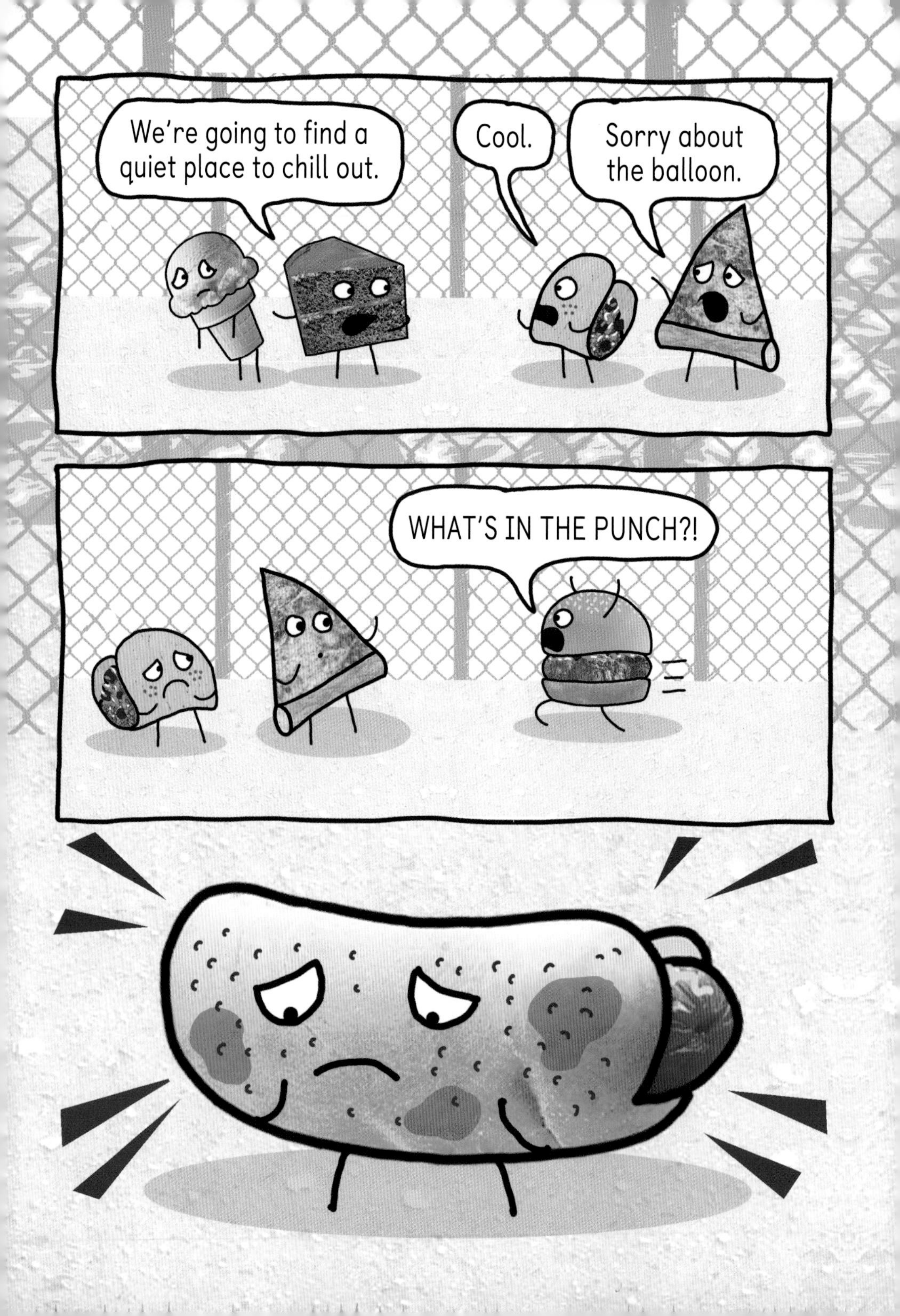

We're going to find a quiet place to chill out.
Cool.
Sorry about the balloon.
WHAT'S IN THE PUNCH?!

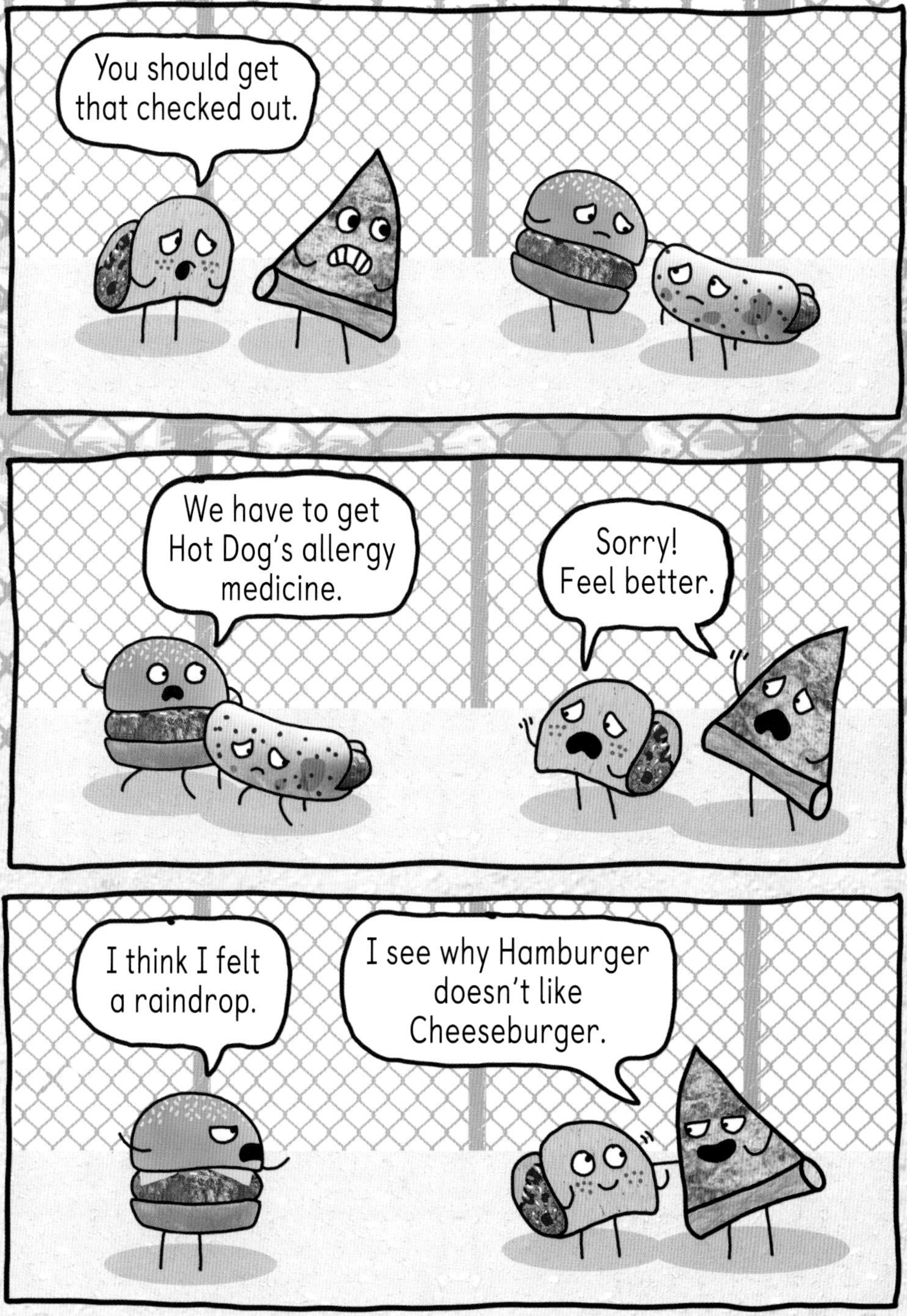
You should get that checked out.
We have to get Hot Dog's allergy medicine.
Sorry! Feel better.
I think I felt a raindrop.
I see why Hamburger doesn't like Cheeseburger.

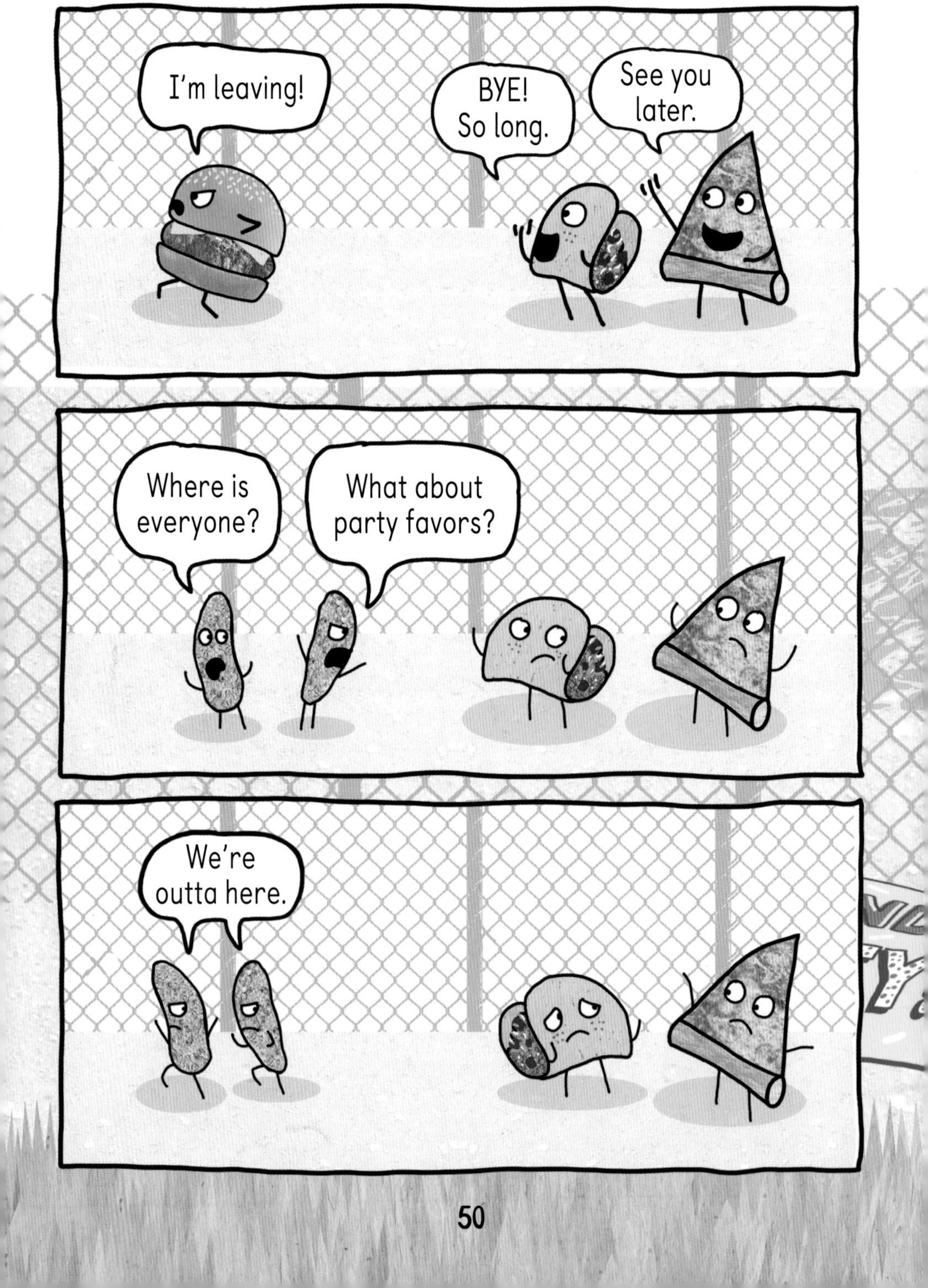
I'm leaving!
BYE! So long.
See you later.
Where is everyone?
What about party favors?
We're outta here.

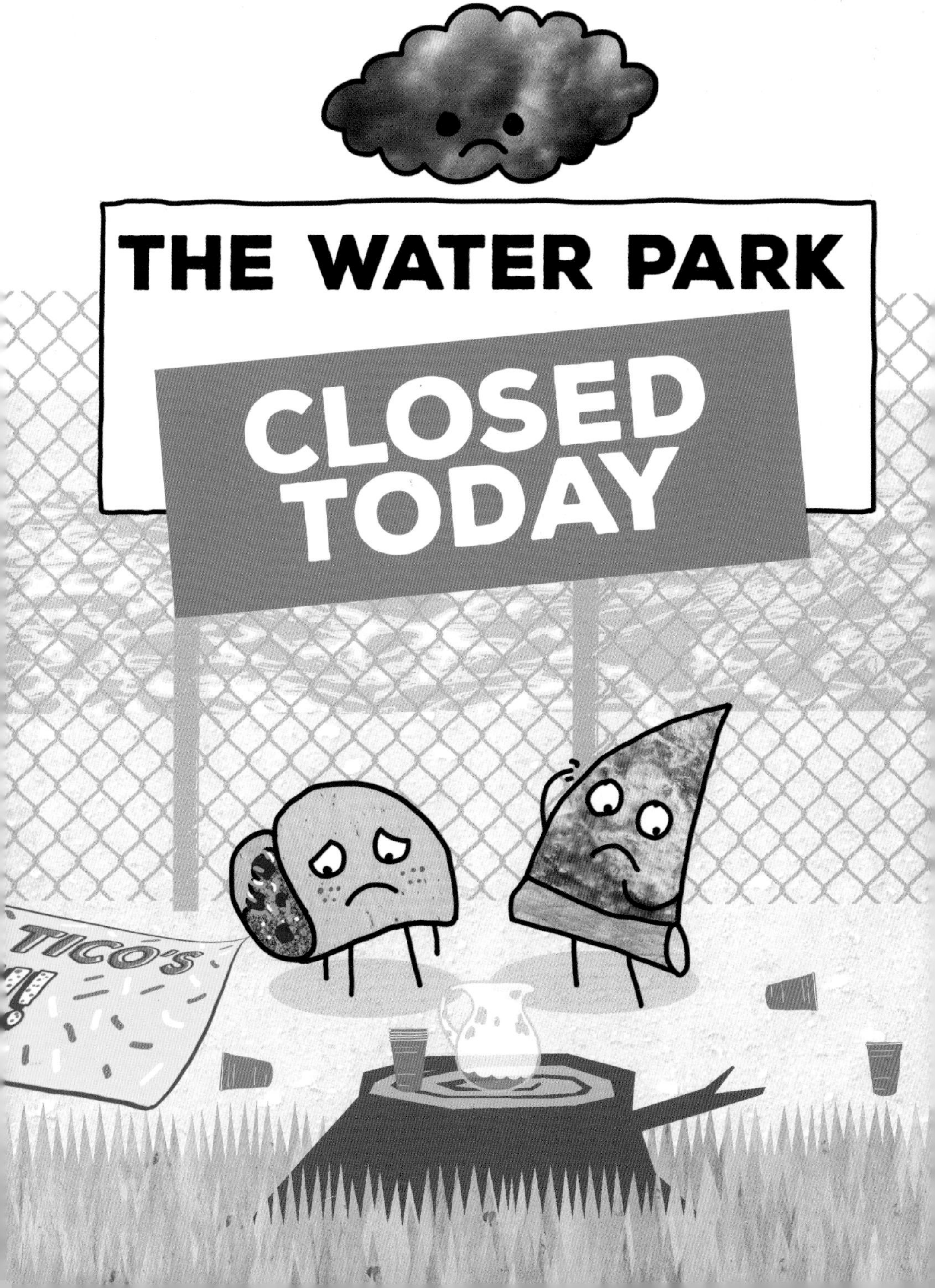
THE WATER PARK
CLOSED TODAY
TICO'S

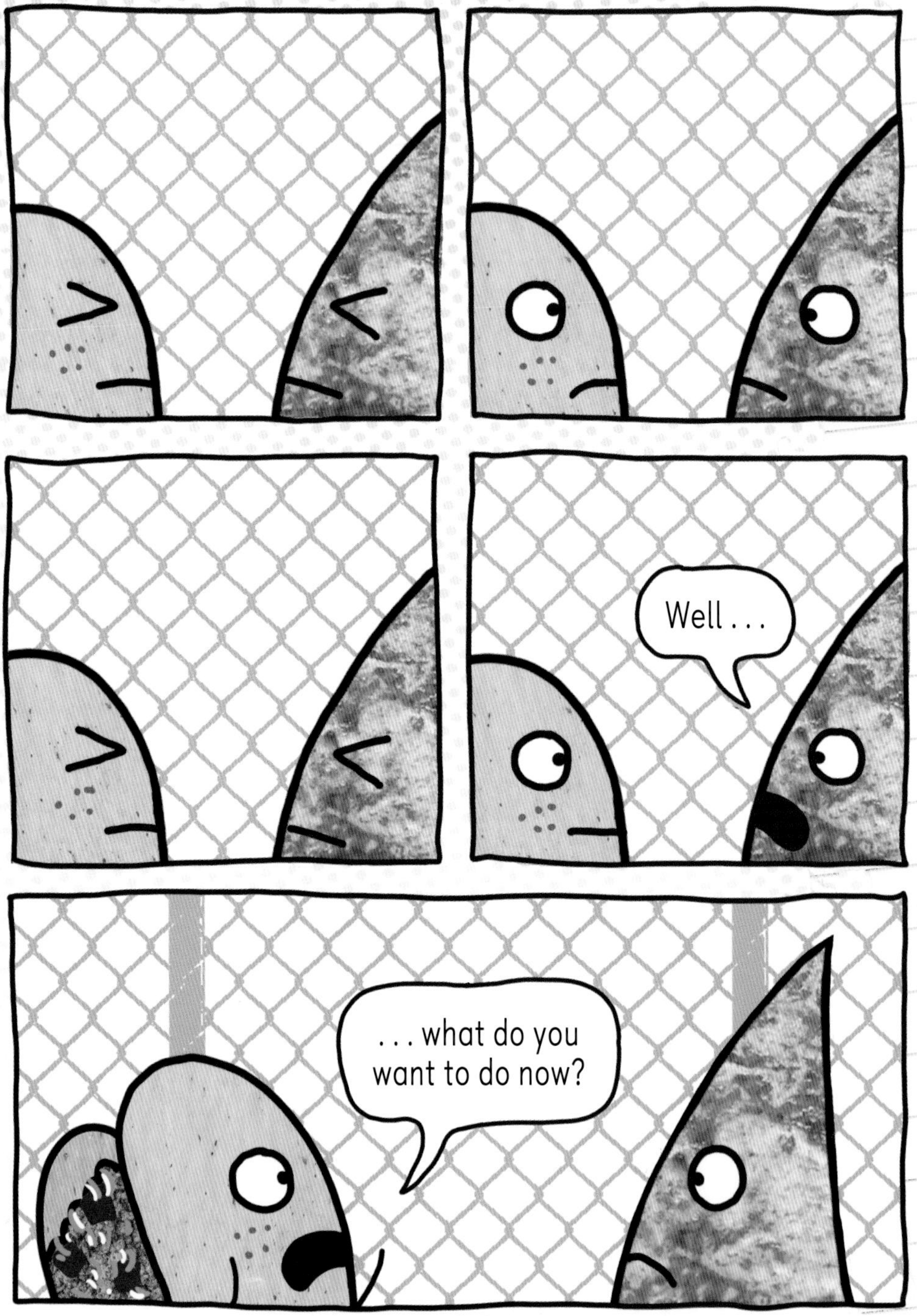
Well . . .
. . . what do you want to do now?

Chapter 5
What Do You
Want to Do Now?

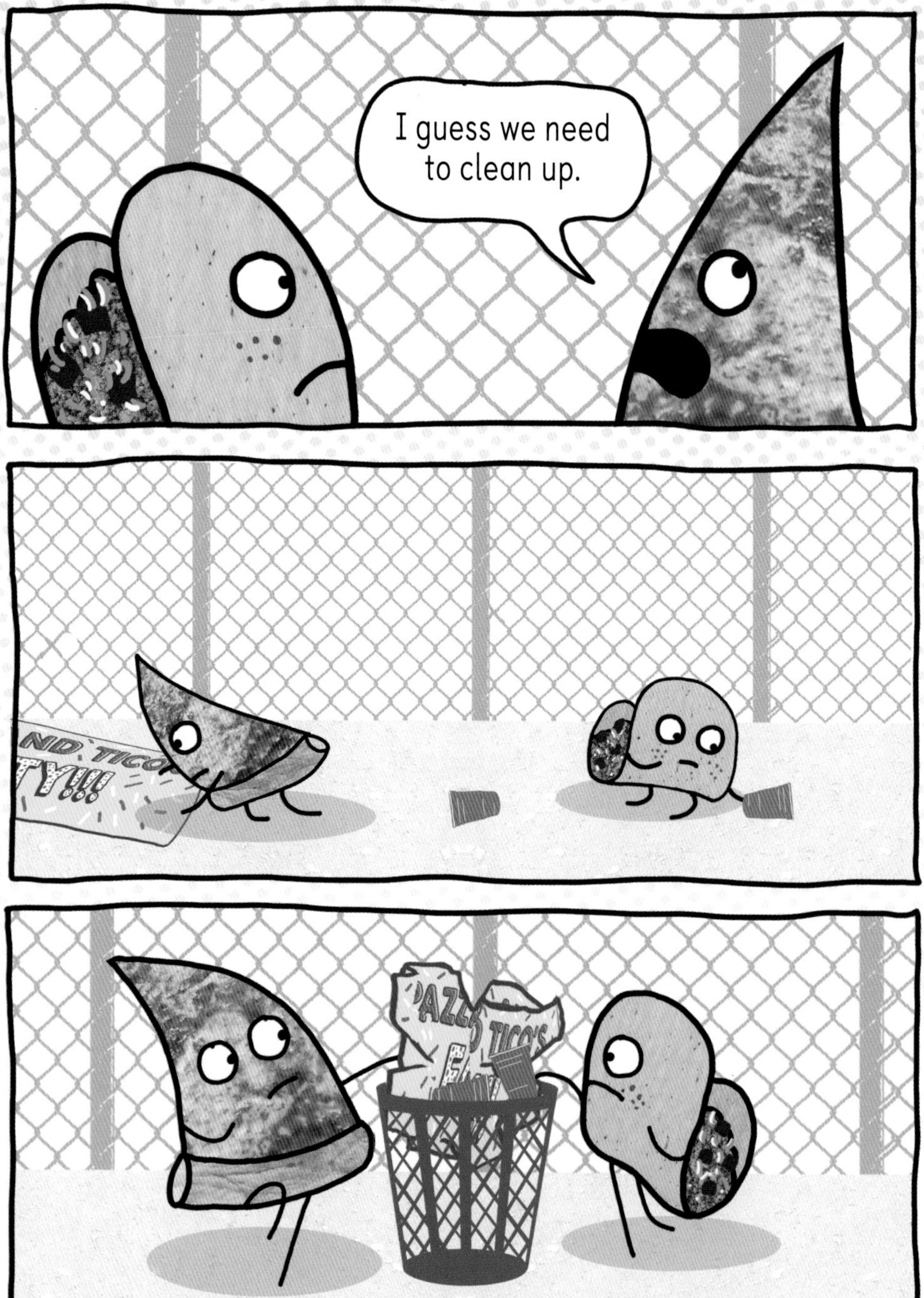
I guess we need to clean up.
ND TICO
TY!!!
TICO'S

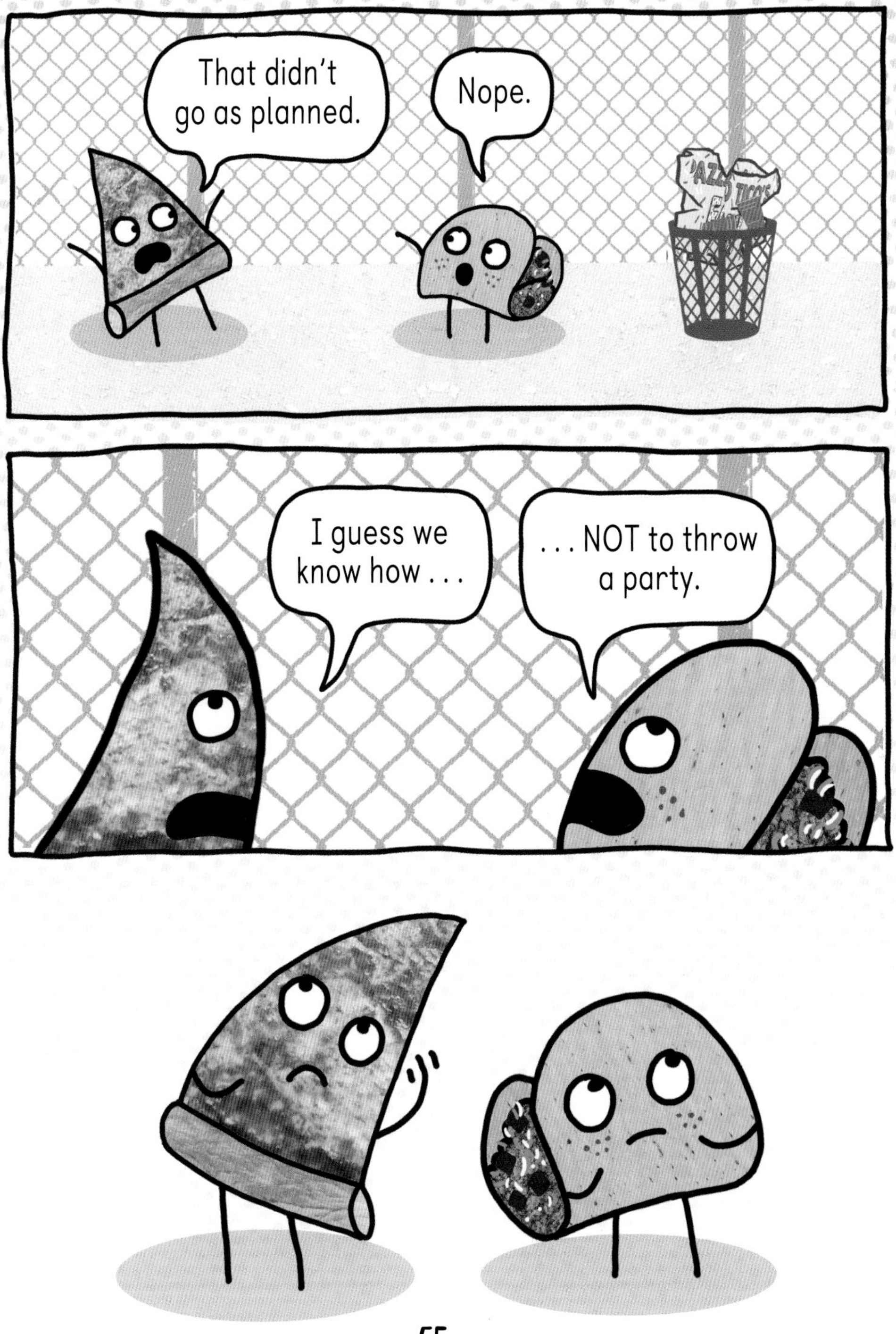
That didn't go as planned.
Nope.
I guess we know how . . .
. . . NOT to throw a party.

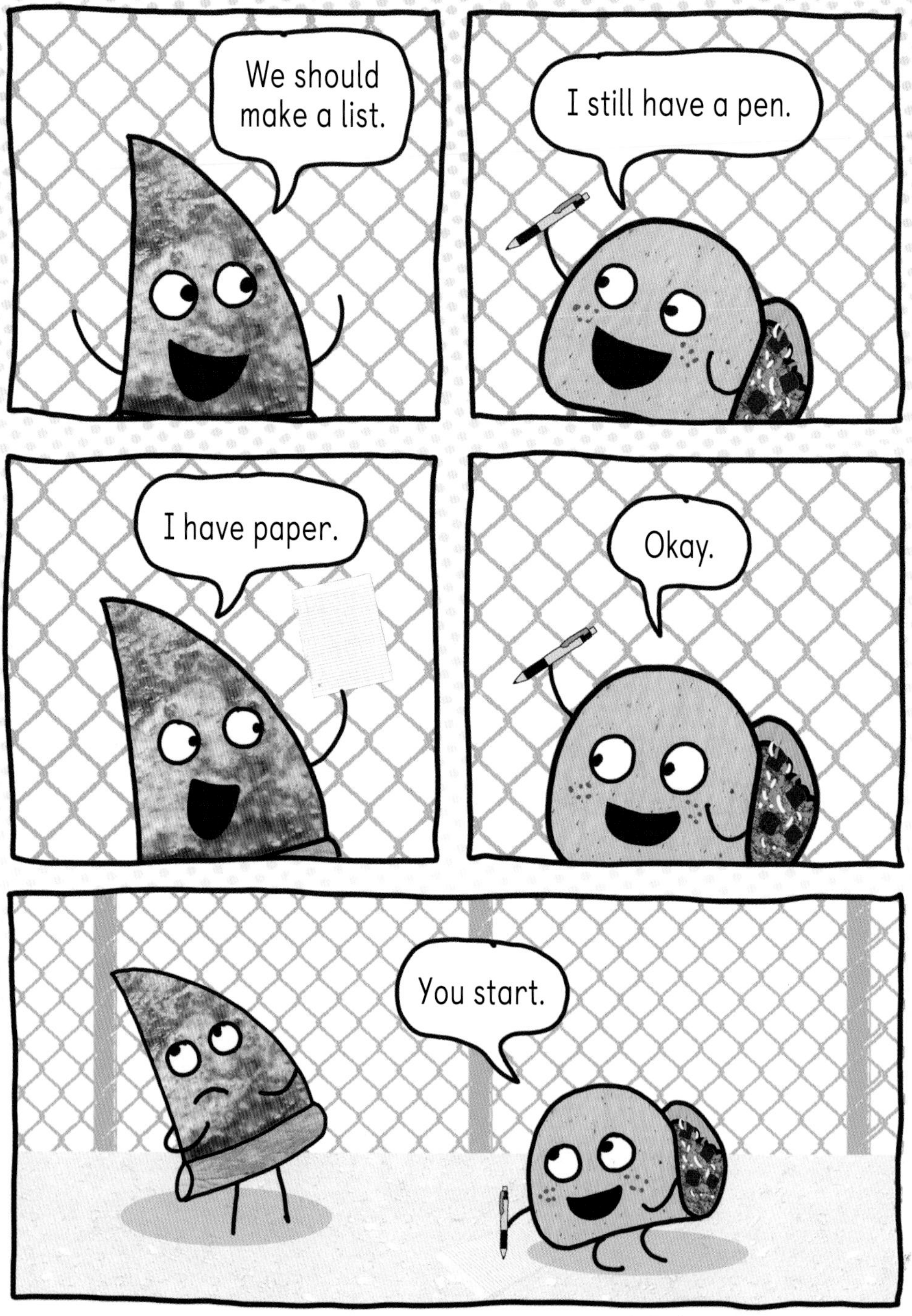
We should make a list.
I still have a pen.
I have paper.
Okay.
You start.

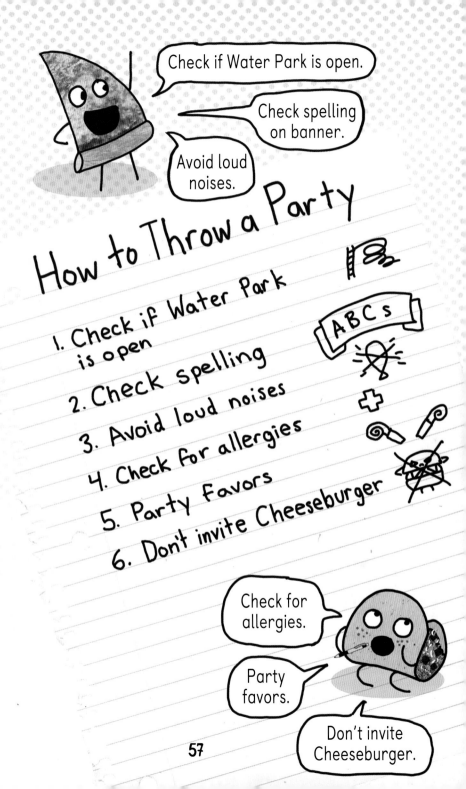

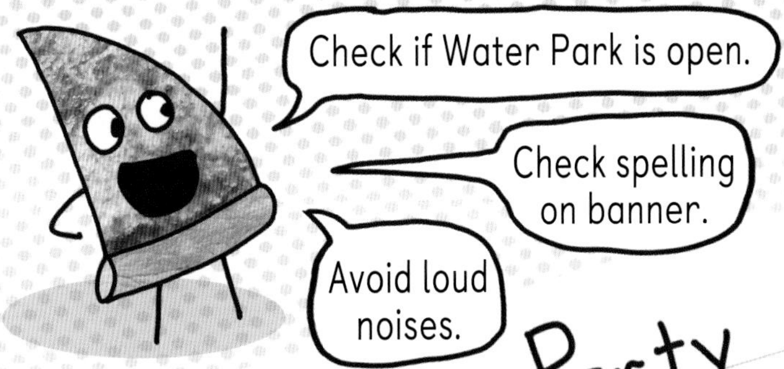
Check if Water Park is open.
Check spelling on banner.
Avoid loud noises.

How to Throw a Party

1. Check if Water Park is open
2. Check spelling
3. Avoid loud noises
4. Check for allergies
5. Party Favors
6. Don't invite Cheeseburger

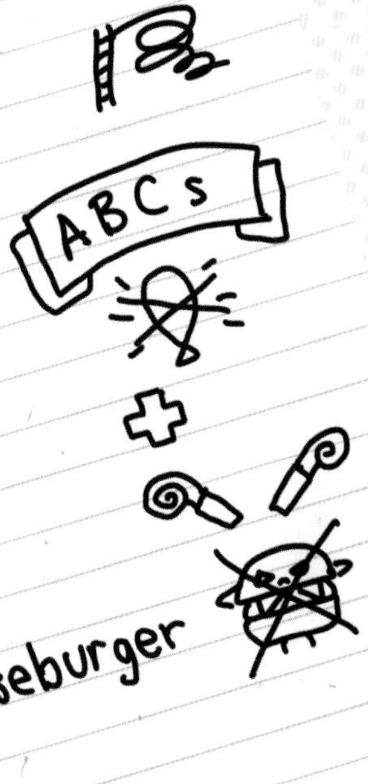
ABCs

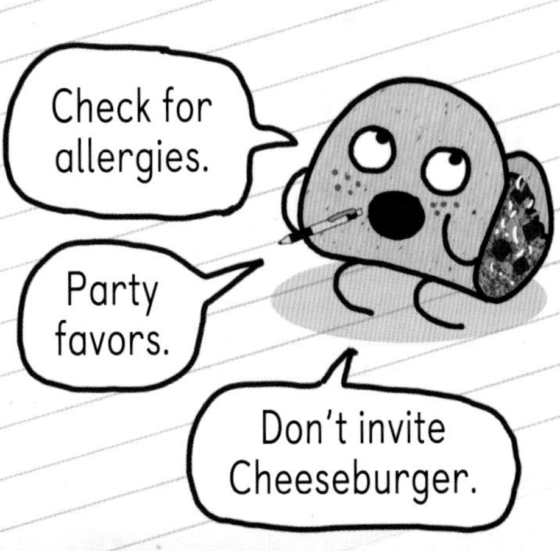
Check for allergies.
Party favors.
Don't invite Cheeseburger.

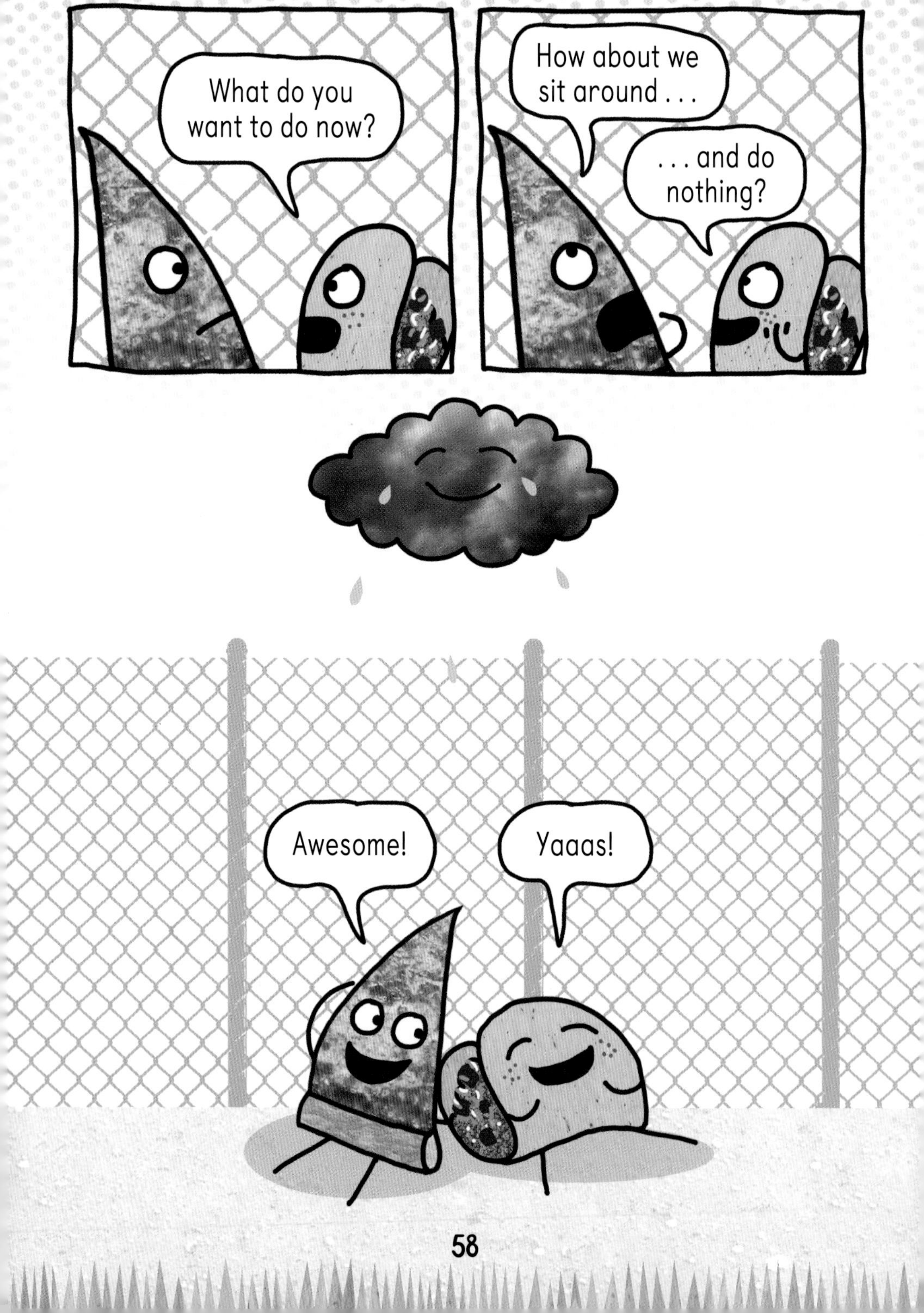
What do you want to do now?
How about we sit around . . .
. . . and do nothing?
Awesome!
Yaaas!

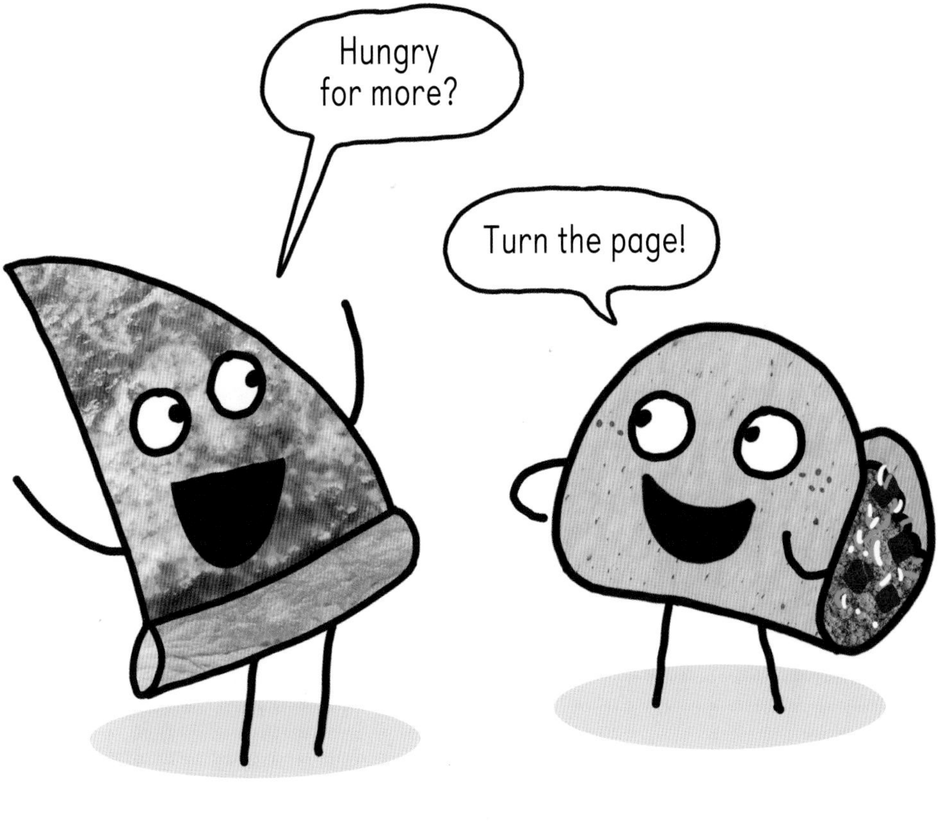
Hungry
for more?
Turn the page!

Par-tay! Yaaas!

Did you enjoy partying with Pizza and Taco?
Then consider yourself INVITED . . .
to read the next book!

What: **PIZZA AND TACO: SUPER-AWESOME COMIC!**

When: Coming in fall 2021!

Where: Wherever books are sold!

Sneak peek!

Taco!
Taco! Taco! Taco!
HEY TACO!!!
TACO!!!
Oh hey, Pizza.
What cha doing?
I'M MAKING A COMIC!

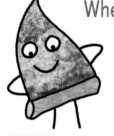

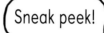

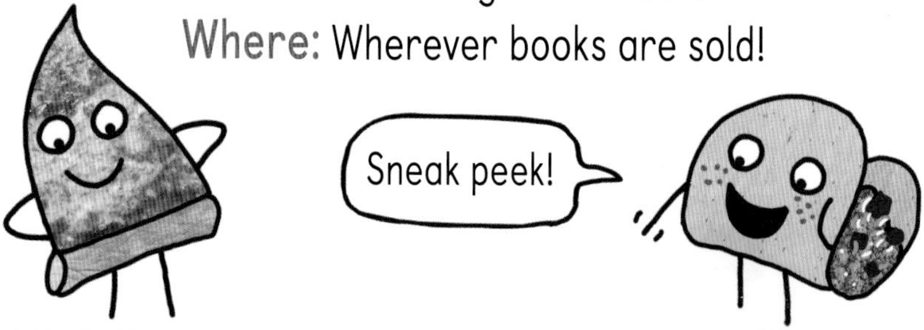

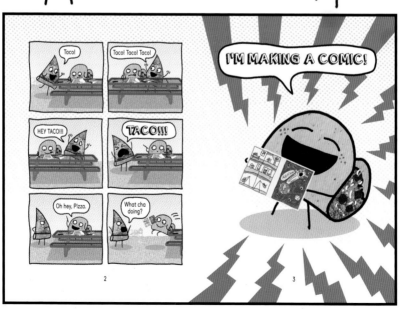

AWESOME COMICS FOR AWESOME KIDS

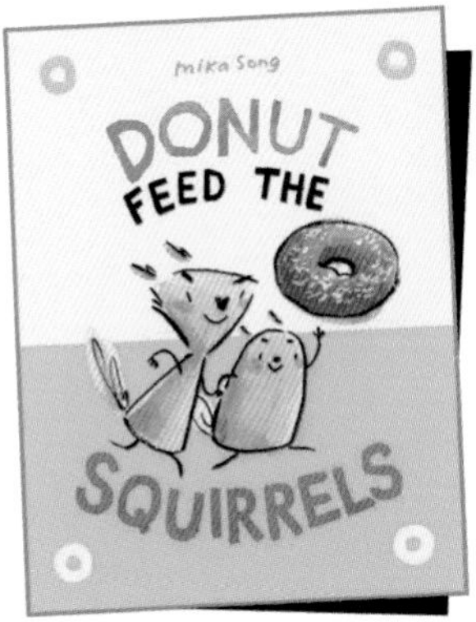
Mika Song
DONUT FEED THE SQUIRRELS

DONUT FEED THE SQUIRRELS

What will these squirrels do for the chance to eat the perfect donut?

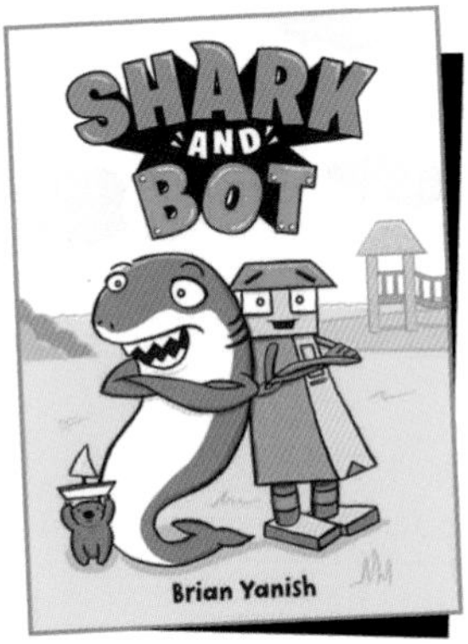
SHARK AND BOT
Brian Yanish

SHARK AND BOT

Will this mismatched pair become best friends forever?

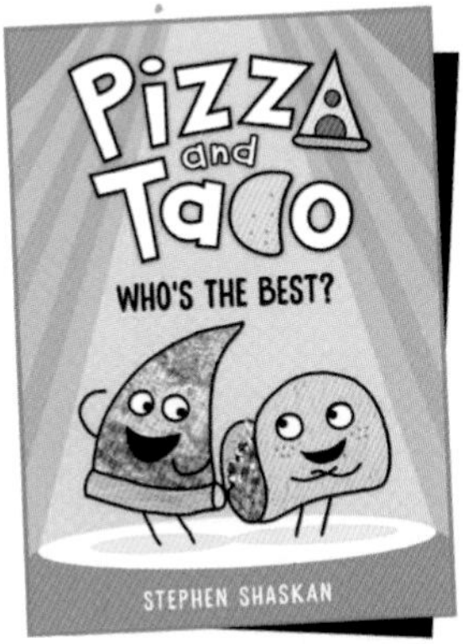
Pizza and Taco
WHO'S THE BEST?
STEPHEN SHASKAN

PIZZA AND TACO

Who's the best? Find out with food, friends, and waterslides.

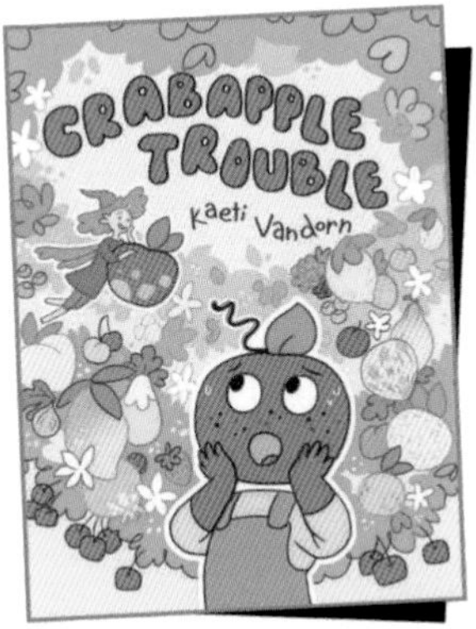
CRABAPPLE TROUBLE
Kaeti Vandorn

CRABAPPLE TROUBLE

Join Calla and Thistle as they face their fears in this magical adventure!

RH GRAPHIC

VISIT US AT RHKIDSGRAPHIC.COM

@RHKIDSGRAPHIC

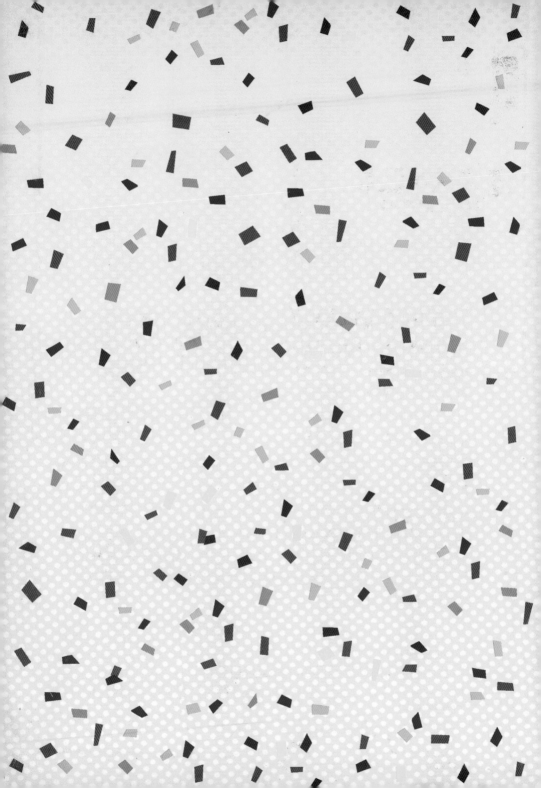